I'm the VILLAINESS, so I'm Taming the Final Boss

1

Sarasa Nagase

ILLUSTRATION BY
Mai Murasaki

YEN ON

New York

I'M THE VILLAINESS, SO I'M TAMING THE FINAL BOSS, Vol. 1
Sarasa Nagase

Translation by Taylor Engel
Cover art by Mai Murasaki

AKUYAKU REIJO NANODE LAST BOSS O KATTE MIMASHITA
©Sarasa Nagase 2017
First published in Japan in 2017 by KADOKAWA CORPORATION, Tokyo.
English translation rights arranged with KADOKAWA CORPORATION, Tokyo, through TUTTLE-MORI AGENCY, INC., Tokyo.

English translation © 2021 by Yen Press, LLC

Yen On
150 West 30th Street, 19th Floor
New York, NY 10001

Visit us at yenpress.com
facebook.com/yenpress
twitter.com/yenpress
yenpress.tumblr.com
instagram.com/yenpress

First Yen On Edition: September 2021

Yen On is an imprint of Yen Press, LLC.
The Yen On name and logo are trademarks of Yen Press, LLC.

Library of Congress Cataloging-in-Publication Data
Names: Nagase, Sarasa, author. | Murasaki, Mai, illustrator. | Engel, Taylor, translator.
Title: I'm the villainess, so I'm taming the final boss / Sarasa Nagase ;
    illustration by Mai Murasaki ; translation by Taylor Engel.
Other titles: Akuyaku reijou nanode last boss wo kattemimashita. English
Description: First Yen On edition. | New York, NY : Yen On, 2021
Identifiers: LCCN 2021030963 | ISBN 9781975334055 (v. 1 ; trade paperback)
Subjects: LCGFT: Fantasy fiction. | Light novels.
Classification: LCC PL873.5.A246 A7913 2021 | DDC 895.63/6—dc23
LC record available at https://lccn.loc.gov/2021030963

ISBNs: 978-1-9753-3405-5 (paperback)
        978-1-9753-3406-2 (ebook)

10 9 8 7 6 5 4 3 2 1

LSC-C

Printed in the United States of America

I'm the VILLAINESS, So I'm
Taming the Final Boss

CONTENTS

I'm the VILLAINESS, So I'm Taming the Final Boss

Character Introductions and Glossary

Claude Jean Ellmeyer

The demon king and oldest prince of Imperial Ellmeyer. The source of Aileen's death flags.

Aileen Lauren d'Autriche

A reincarnated villainess. Due to the shock of having her engagement broken, she's regained memories of her past life.

Keith

Claude's childhood friend
and human attendant.

Beelzebuth

A demon who idolizes Claude
and has pledged to obey him.

Cedric Jean Ellmeyer

The hero of the game. Breaks
off his engagement to Aileen.

Lilia Reinoise

The heroine of the game.
Cedric's beloved.

The *otome* game *Regalia of Saints, Demons, and Maidens*

A game set in the Ellmeyer Empire, a country vaguely modeled on the kingdoms of Western Europe and where the legend of the Maid of the Sacred Sword is still told. It's also the world that Aileen was reincarnated into. In the game, Cedric's route is the default one. Over the course of the route, Lilia discovers she is the reincarnation of the Maid of the Sacred Sword and eventually becomes a saint who saves the country. The enemy the Maid must defeat is Claude, who awakens as the final boss.

Come to think of it, I've often had curious dreams ever since I was small. Dreams in which I become someone I don't know, someone who spends her time all alone, in a white room that smells of disinfectant, playing with a device whose workings are a complete mystery.

Since they are dreams, I can't recall the details. Even my own name is unclear. However...

"Honestly, child. You're always playing that game."

The daydreams replay behind my eyes at a furious pace. My body tilts dizzily, and then I'm on my hands and knees on the cold, hard floor.

It feels as if I've suddenly remembered the exact whereabouts of something I'd forgotten. A great wave of information crashes over me, and my head throbs violently.

At last, my eyes focus on the marble floor. Its surface has been polished until it shines, and I can see my reflection in it—or at least, I think that's what my eyes are telling me.

But who is this splendid beauty, with hair like spun gold and mystical sapphire eyes? With pale fingers, I trace the slender neck up to the oval outline of the face.

This face… I feel as if I saw it in the game… What? "Game"?

When I blink, the long eyelashes rise and fall. Someone is standing directly in front of me.

It's a golden-haired youth. His lips are twisted, and he's looking down at me.

"Making a show of kneeling and weeping won't win you any sympathy. Everyone here knows: You constantly did as you pleased, taking full advantage of your position as my betrothed. No one has any reason to sympathize with you."

"—Master…Cedric? Are you truly Master Cedric?"

My voice is faint and trembling. The blond, princely youth's response sounds ironic.

"I expect you're trying to say this is strange coming from me. This is who I truly am, though. You were my fiancée for years, and you never even saw that."

A pang runs through my chest, and I slowly come to grips with reality.

That's right; this is reality. The person in front of me is Cedric Jean Ellmeyer, crown prince of Imperial Ellmeyer. I've known him since we were very young. He is my fiancé—and a love interest in the game that I adored.

…Game? Love interest?

Bewildered by my own memories, I look around. All I see are cold, piercing eyes.

This evening, the academy I attend is holding a soiree in celebration of the end of the winter term. The teachers have all excused themselves, and only students are present now… And yet every single one of them is watching me coldly from a distance.

The only one whose eyes seem to contain pity for me is the girl who's nestled close to Cedric. Her name is Lilia Reinoise.

Although of common birth, she's now the daughter of a baron and quite popular here at school.

Silky caramel-colored hair, supple cheeks, lips that look so sweet. Right now, her large eyes are filled with concern for me.

I'd expect no less of a heroine, I think, looking up at her. Then suddenly, it occurs to me.

In that case, I must be...

"Aileen Lauren d'Autriche. I'm dissolving our engagement."

"—Wait, that's...!"

That's my name. And also the name of the game's villainess.

Wait, wait, wait! That's right; Master Cedric is my fiancé...which means I'm...

I've been watching my current situation unfold as if it has no bearing on me, but all at once, I begin to think about it. Seeing Aileen so clearly anxious, Cedric sneers at her.

"I've decided to be true to myself and live my life with Lilia."

"...Lady Aileen, I'm sorry."

What do you mean, you're "sorry"?

The violent emotion surging up from the depths of my throat is, properly speaking, *Aileen's.*

My vision grows misty again, but I bite my lip, trying to stay in control. I take another look at myself.

I'm sitting weakly on the floor, in a magnificent dress made of layer upon layer of lace. It's an unladylike state, completely unsuitable for the daughter of a duke. However, no one offers me a helping hand.

After all, this is the "villainess's broken engagement" event.

"I'm sick to death of your deluded belief that I love you."

Why did you smile and say you loved me as I was, then?

The words are pathetic, and I bite them back. They feel as

heavy as lead, but strangely, once I've swallowed them, my heart grows calmer.

...*How should I put this? I do think my memories have chosen an awful time to come back...but it's helped me collect myself just a little.*

Enough that I can understand that I've been well and truly used and tossed aside.

"If you have anything to say in your defense, I won't refuse to listen."

If this had happened when I still knew nothing, I'm sure I would have fought tooth and nail. I would have been fighting the wrong person.

That thought gives me room to breathe. Smiling thinly, I raise my head.

"No, Master Cedric— Although, I do think that had you been honest with me in the first place, there would have been no need to prepare such an exaggerated venue, nor to cause such a scene."

When I gaze coldly at those around me, some of the onlookers quickly avert their eyes, possibly because they've taken my meaning. However, Cedric simply responds with a snort.

"We're demonstrating our resolution, Lilia and I."

"It's not because you were frightened that should you have chosen some other public place, you would have been reprimanded by both the house of d'Autriche and the emperor?"

"Of course not. I simply felt that your crimes should be judged before everyone."

"My crimes? Wha—?!!"

Suddenly, someone beside me pulls my arm, lifting me. Turning my head, I look at my opponent.

"Refrain from manhandling me, if you would. Is that any way to treat a lady?"

"What 'lady'?! Enough of this, Aileen. There's no way to disguise what you've done."

It's another childhood friend of mine who's spoken, Marcus Cowell. He shoves a sheaf of papers under my nose. He's a slim, taciturn young man who is seen as the likely future captain of the knights. He has a strong sense of justice, and he will not countenance unfairness. He glowers with his intimidating eyes at me, as if I'm a criminal.

"...I'm perfectly capable of standing on my own. Unhand me, won't you?"

I gaze back at Marcus coldly, rise to my feet without any help, and pull my arm free. I then flip through the papers that he's held out to me. They're written accusations. When did he collect these?

Because Lilia is of lower rank, I bullied her by telling her not to speak to me first. At my insistence, the play for the academy festival was changed, and poor Lilia was forced to learn her lines all over again. I threatened that if she didn't do as I told her, I'd have her bureaucrat parents demoted— And so on and so forth, for pages.

All the statements are anonymous, and naturally, none are signed. Running out of patience, I toss them away behind me.

"Ridiculous. You call this proof?"

In the midst of a cloud of rustling, drifting paper, I smile elegantly.

"Marcus. Let me enlighten you. 'So-and-so says such and such' isn't proof. It's merely rumor, or possibly libel."

"—! Even with all these reports, you deny it?! Don't think you can get away with this just because you're the daughter of Duke d'Autriche!"

"My, I do believe you've taken me for a fool. If Duke d'Autriche's daughter tried in earnest to cover something up, do you really believe there would be any proof left to find? Besides, could this whole farce be any more juvenile? When did the students of this academy regress to infancy?"

As I speak, I grind one of the papers that's fallen to the velvet carpet under the toe of my shoe. Then I smile.

"If you insist that I look these over, would you collect them once more and with signatures? If you do, I'll make certain to remember them—every single name. Surely, you aren't telling me they require anonymity in order to accuse a mere girl like myself? What a disgrace that would be."

Irritated by my choice of words, Marcus spits out his response.

"Why is that you can speak so glibly while even the idea of apologizing never occurs to you?"

"Apologize? Yes, in that case, I shall. Lady Lilia. As you were raised a commoner, I do apologize for attempting to force you to abide by the aristocratic rule that one must not speak to those of higher rank unless spoken to first. I also regret that I had the school play changed out of concern that it would be difficult for you to learn such lengthy lines."

"Hold your tongue, Aileen! Have you not ridiculed Lilia enough?!"

I'm the one who's being ridiculed. The crown prince himself has just informed me, in front of an audience, that he is breaking off our engagement. He's even collected infantile written accusations in order to prove beyond doubt that everyone hates me. If they had no intention of collectively making a laughingstock of me, there would've been no need for any of this.

However, it's likely that Cedric, red-faced and angry, and

Marcus, who's trembling with clenched fists, see only Lilia, whose eyes are damp with tears. Upon closer inspection, I realize that the students at the very front of the crowd are other love interests and their hangers-on.

Attendance was not mandatory at this soiree. They must have deliberately organized to make this moment come together. After waiting for the teachers to depart, they sprung their trap.

How wily of them— No, however it happened, I'm the one who was outplayed.

It's pointless to stay here any longer. I sigh at the futility of it all, then take a deep breath.

"This has gone on long enough. I'll be taking my leave, then. My only regret is that I can't shamefully weep and beg for you, as I'm sure many of those assembled here had hoped I would."

Bite back the tears. Only show a smile. The last thing I want is to allow them to feel even a hint of superiority at having caught me in their little scheme.

That means I have to be the one to bring the curtain down.

"On that note, good evening, everyone. Master Cedric—I did admire you."

Cedric looks as if that parting comment caught him by surprise.

However, I've already put all of it behind me. With impeccable manners, I raise the hem of my skirt and curtsy. Then I gracefully leave the hall, turning my back on its glimmering chandeliers.

Possibly because I've gritted my teeth in a stubborn refusal to cry, my temples are throbbing. Even so, I force myself to think.

In the game, after this point, I will be expelled from the academy at Cedric's request, because he "doesn't even want to see my face." If that's how it's going to play out, I'll simply withdraw voluntarily before that happens. The game ends with the academy's graduation ceremony. That's still about three months away. I'll have to use my remaining time efficiently.

If I recall correctly, there were several other major events leading up to that. My memories are still a jumble, and a lot of it is vague, but I'm fairly sure that the ducal family disowned Aileen. She was turned out into the town's seedier district and fell into self-destructive ways.

That's right. If this really is the world of the game, I don't have a moment to waste on tears.

Three months from now, during the "ending," by the time everyone else is graduating from the academy, Aileen the villainess will be dead.

"That isn't even funny."

I won't give them the satisfaction of seeing me cry. I won't give up. I refuse to die for the happiness of people like them.

Think. Remember. What can I do under these circumstances…? Then it hits me. I gasp, eyes widening.

"…They do say *The enemy of my enemy is my friend*, don't they?"

A smile that doesn't go past my tense rouged lips slowly appears.

That smile makes me look every bit a villainous young noblewoman, but at least I manage to not cry.

✦ First Act ✦
The Villainess Could Not Care Less
If She Is Unpopular

Wings rustling, crows as dark as pitch take flight, rising into the night sky.

As Aileen ducks, black cats cross her path.

It's a veritable parade of ill omens. However, Aileen walks without hesitation through these woods, late at night with only a hand lantern for light, her chin tucked in. In her other hand, she carries a slender sword.

With a rustle of leaves, an enormous rat darts out of the brush and comes to a stop. It glares up at Aileen with its single large eye. Its ears are abnormally big, and sharp fangs jut from its mouth.

...A demon. You almost never see them in the first layer, but...

When she turns the lantern's light on it, the demon-rat plunges into the bushes on the opposite side of the path, vanishing. With a sigh of relief, she gets a better grip on her sword, but just as she's about to start walking again, she notices something.

"Crows...? I wonder why they're all perched on skulls. Don't tell me they're demons as well."

Not only that, but there are also scores of them in the tops of the dead trees, looking down at her. If they all attack her at once, she probably— No, she definitely won't escape unscathed.

Their cawing almost sounds as if they're discussing how best to do away with her.

Dealing with this many would be a bit much... No, I mustn't lose heart. If I turn back here, I'll die.

Although, that might still happen even if she presses on.

"Technically, the Maid of the Sacred Sword's blood does run in my veins. Wouldn't that qualify as falling under her protection? In any case, I doubt I'll die until *that time* comes..."

How ironic. The fact that she's destined to die later on guarantees there's nothing to be afraid of now. With a self-deprecating smile, she raises the lantern. At the end of the path revealed by the spilling light, she sees an old, dilapidated building.

It's a royal estate that fell out of use long ago—an abandoned castle.

If the rumors are correct, and if this really is the same world as that game, then the person she's after lives in those ruins beyond the dense forest.

"Turn back."

When a large crow utters that warning, Aileen shrinks back. Apparently, they talk. Turns out they really are demons.

Seizing the opportunity, the crows surrounding her cry out.

"Turn back, human."

"Up ahead is the demon king's castle."

"The demon king is reading."

Though it certainly seems strange for the crows to mix in oddly calming tidbits of information, she can't find it in her to laugh in a situation where birds are talking to her.

"Why are you here, girl? In a rush to get killed?"

"Her engagement got called off yesterday. Come for revenge, have you? Pointless."

She flinches, scowling. The crows caw, jeering at her.

"How come she looks like she doesn't care even when everyone hates her?"

"The girl talks a big game, but she's pathetic. Pathetic!"

"Your reputation is ruined. Selfish, snobby damaged goods—"

"...Insulting your visitors out of the blue? Is that how you lot do things around here?"

Aileen glares at the crows, her gaze steady. She stands tall and wears an easy, elegant smile.

"Did you collect those rumors on orders from the demon king? I must admit I'm rather surprised that he has such vulgar taste."

Every crow eyes her angrily. Demons hold the demon king in the highest regard. A slight against him is a slight against them all. And taunting them is suicide.

However, carrying herself like a hero on her way to challenge the demon king, Aileen issues a bold declaration.

"I apologize for my discourtesy in calling unannounced at this hour. However, if Master Claude Jean Ellmeyer proves to be petty enough to base his decisions on mere hearsay, I will promptly take my leave. Now settle down, will you?"

Ending her remark with a smile, Aileen gracefully walks on. For some reason, the crows keep their silence. Taking flight, they fall in behind her as she follows the trail through the gloomy forest. When she glances over, there's a rustling in the bushes that seems to be tailing her as well.

Failure is unacceptable. That is what Aileen has been taught, and so she ignores everything stalking her and presses on.

Before long, the view opens up.

Under a starless sky, the abandoned castle appears. The

structure itself is on the verge of crumbling in several places. What tapestries that remain hanging are soot stained and tattered, and many of its vine-tangled pillars lie broken. The surrounding trees are withered and lifeless, while the small pond nearby is clouded and dark, having transformed into a bottomless swamp. The crows fly ahead of Aileen, creating a foreboding atmosphere that feels terribly appropriate.

This is the demon king's castle.

The imposing silhouette revealed by the lantern's light makes her gulp audibly.

It's all right. He's supposed to turn out to be a kind person... But what if that's only true for the heroine? That's totally possible.

Wishful thinking is the enemy. Aileen has little choice but to steel herself and go. She takes a deep breath and raises her head.

As she continues forward, she passes a stump that's surrounded by what appear to be scattered human bones. After finally reaching the rusted iron door, she pushes with all her might, but it shows no sign of moving. Panting, she tries again and again, but it refuses to budge.

Still, she can't just give up now. As she raises her hands again, someone speaks up behind her.

"Let me help you."

"My. That's very kind of—"

With a roar, the iron door is blown away. The polite smile Aileen has reflexively assumed freezes up. She turns to get a look at the one who's blasted the door away with the tip of a single finger.

The lantern's light casts a deep shadow.

Lustrous black hair of a shade deeper than the surrounding

darkness streams in the damp night wind, revealing the man's features. She remembers what he looks like, or at least thought she did, but when she lays eyes on his living face, its diabolical beauty takes her breath away.

A straight, neat nose and thin lips. Everything, from his features to his frame, is as perfectly sculpted as a first-class work of art. However, what's most striking is his bloodred eyes.

H-he's way more impressive in person than as a static image...!

But she *does* know this face. That fact alone strengthens her resolve.

Aileen has no time. The broken engagement is an event flag on the Cedric route. At this rate, unless she does something drastic, she'll die.

Without ever getting a proper chance to love, dream, or even enjoy her old age. Just like how she frivoled away her past life.

"What business does a human have with me?"

Claude Jean Ellmeyer, demon king and oldest prince of the Ellmeyer Empire, speaks with absolutely no emotion in his red eyes. Only his lips move.

I can't lose my nerve after coming this far. Aileen draws herself up as she runs her fingers through her hair and flashes her usual smile.

"It's nothing unpleasant. I've come to propose to you."

Right around the moment she starts to wonder why he isn't reacting, lightning falls from the sky, splitting a great, dead tree cleanly in two and setting it ablaze. It's almost as if she's provoked the wrath of the gods.

"......"

"Who...is proposing marriage...to whom?"

Aileen's smile has frozen up. Her question has just been

politely turned back on her. Behind him, leaping flames crackle, illuminating their surroundings. It's rather reminiscent of a scene from hell.

However, even though she's faltered, she points at him, determined not to lose.

"A-as I said, I am proposing to you—!"

When lightning strikes around her three times in a row, the courage she mustered gives way to her instincts, and before she has a chance to hear his response, Aileen keels over and faints.

The shock of being jilted by my fiancé has caused me to remember my past life.

If she'd said a thing like that, either her overprotective older brothers would have summoned a physician, or her mother would have told her that she clearly hadn't trained enough and then ship her off to do drills.

As such, last night—after returning home, alone and miserable—Aileen decided to spend her time reviewing in her mind everything that had happened that day. Fortunately, when she told her family she was feeling unwell and wouldn't need dinner, they quite naturally assumed she was in low spirits because her engagement had been called off so unceremoniously. They said discussion of the future could wait until things had settled down and then left her to her own devices.

Thanks to that, it had been a simple matter to leave undetected. Even if it was late at night, when it came to slipping out of the mansion, the d'Autriche household's outstanding servants were always formidable opponents. The words *Just let her be* had never proved so useful as they did that night.

In the first place, if it became known that she had gone to the demon king's castle right on the heels of the current commotion, it would have ruined what reputation she had left.

My brothers are inclined to spoil me, but they show no mercy. And Father is, well...

Her name is Aileen Lauren d'Autriche.

That is who she currently is. The sole daughter of the house of d'Autriche, the greatest noble family in the Ellmeyer Empire, linked to the imperial family by blood. Her father is the prime minister, while her mother holds the title of duchess and is the highly regarded niece of the empress dowager, commanding respect in both high society and the military. Aileen's three older brothers fill out the rest of her family.

As the youngest child and the only daughter, Aileen has been treasured her whole life. The way her brothers dote on her is particularly notorious. However, Aileen knows it's because she is a girl and not as brilliant as her siblings. It's clear they never considered her a rival, a real threat.

She has often felt left out, and no matter how hard she studied, all her brothers consistently outstripped her. It has always seemed impossible to catch up to them in any field. Whenever Aileen sulked, her mother would tell her the same thing, time and time again: *"Women have their own ways of fighting."*

Aileen only realized what she'd meant the year she turned eight. That was when Cedric Jean Ellmeyer, a genuine prince, had knelt before her and asked for her hand in marriage.

Frankly, she'd been overjoyed. Cedric was simply wonderful, and the mere thought that he needed her seemed to give her a special sort of value.

Whoever married him would become empress, and her father

impressed upon her what an achievement it would be to obtain that special title and position.

This was the first expectation that had ever been placed on Aileen, and it soon became her dream to meet it.

She quickly took to studying etiquette and dance while drilling everything from economics to statecraft into her mind, all so that she would be of use to her future husband. Going so far as to prepare for hypothetical situations in which she was, for example, attacked by bandits, she even honed her skill with the sword to keep herself from being a burden.

Aileen was confident that once she was capable in a wide array of fields, Cedric would surely come to rely on her. Everyone would praise her for her efforts. Just thinking about the day that would come true filled her with happiness, and so she redoubled her efforts.

As she dedicated herself to her mission, somewhere along the way, she'd become known as "the arrogant girl who lords over everyone because she's the crown prince's fiancée."

Aileen has always been stubborn and competitive enough to vie with her older brothers. It isn't in her to yield when she's confident she is in the right, and she never hesitated to say what was on her mind. Naturally, her personality has often been the cause of misunderstandings. Her belief in Cedric's shallow remark that he understood her, as well as her resulting neglect of everyone else around her, had been ill-advised.

In no time at all, she became the most hated person at the academy, and Cedric, the one person she was sure truly understood her, did the unthinkable and broke off their engagement.

If Aileen had adopted a slightly more amicable attitude and pretended to be a delicate, frail maiden, then perhaps things might have played out differently. At this point, she's still capable of thinking about it objectively, if only just barely.

This is only because she knows, through the game, exactly how people see her and why.

I do think I neglected what others thought of me... That said, I'm not about to try to patch things up now. After all, even if my memories of my past life have returned, I am no one but myself.

In any case, she could only remember dreamlike fragments of that past life.

She once lived in a land known as Japan, where both science and civilization were far more advanced than they are here. However, she had also been sickly to the point where she often spent the better part of the year in bed. Because she died young, unable even to make the most of her adolescence, she doesn't have a great many memories to begin with. That said, the thought she remembers most vividly is *I wanted to enjoy being a teenager, and if possible, I'd like to experience the sort of romance that you see in* otome *games,* so it's clear she'd been a serious gamer.

The one she played particularly heavily was *Regalia of Saints, Demons, and Maidens.* The game was set in Imperial Ellmeyer, a Western European–style kingdom in which the legend of the Maid of the Sacred Sword was still told—the very world in which Aileen now lives.

In the game, Aileen was betrothed to Cedric, the orthodox hero who required incredibly high stats to conquer. Aileen herself had been a typical villainous young noblewoman who flaunted her privileged status as the daughter of a duke, often prancing about with an entourage of hangers-on and generally obstructing the romantic endeavors of the heroine, Lilia. She picked fights with Lilia, who came from a family of commoners, and blatantly harassed her for enrolling in a school that was attended almost exclusively by the children of the aristocracy. As the heroine's conquest of Cedric progressed, he steadily became more and more disgusted by Aileen's behavior until he finally announced he was breaking off their engagement.

As a story in a game, it was comical, but as Aileen's reality, it's no laughing matter.

Worst of all, no matter what happens from this point on, Aileen is fated to die.

Cedric's route was the so-called main route, and it explored the national legend of the Maid of the Sacred Sword. As the story progressed, it became apparent that Lilia was the reincarnation of the Maid, and in the end, she became a saint who saved the very empire itself. However, before that, the demon king awakened as the final boss, the enemy the Maid of the Sacred Sword must destroy.

That demon king is the very person to whom Aileen has just proposed marriage.

Claude Jean Ellmeyer… If her knowledge of the game is still accurate, he should be twenty-five years old, eight years Aileen's senior. He also happens to be Cedric's elder half brother, and the former crown prince of Imperial Ellmeyer.

However, he was born with red eyes and magic that no other humans could wield. According to the tale of the Maid of the Sacred Sword, these are considered proof that he is the reincarnation of the demon king. From the stories Aileen has heard, whenever danger threatens him, a horde of demons appears out of nowhere. More than anything, the demons love him, and if he ordered them to, they would lay down their lives without hesitation. If that's not a demon king, then who could be?

As a young child, Claude was the target of multiple assassination attempts, but every time without fail, demons saved him. At their wits' end, his would-be killers compromised by stripping Claude of his right to inherit the throne and confining him to the abandoned castle, ignoring his very existence.

In most of the game's routes, he awakened as the demon king, standing in the way of the heroine and her chosen love interest. In one ending, he destroyed the empire, while in another, he was slain by the sword that would materialize from Lilia's body. In the ensuing chaos, Aileen died.

Sometimes, she was seared to the bone by the beams of light Claude emitted upon becoming the demon king, and other times, she was offered as a ritual sacrifice to resurrect him. She was also frequently killed off in the narration, like a minor NPC. She was usually treated as an insignificant character throughout most of the game. Aileen's most important appearances happened during the events leading up to the broken engagement; from that point on, it became pretty clear that the staff hadn't consider it worth the effort to revisit her character in detail.

Well, sure, the players aren't likely to complain if she's killed off, but come on—!

As the one who's slated to be killed off, that's just unacceptable. Aileen's fate is so tragic. Admittedly, the way she behaved was problematic.

However, she hardly did anything that warrants death, and really, the idea that a single person is the root of all evil is only plausible in a game.

As she reaches that conclusion, Aileen's consciousness ripples. She can hear voices.

"...So why are you personally caring for a human girl, my king?"

"No particular reason."

"Well, I for one think it's a good thing. Any prince worth his salt should be kind to ladies."

There are three voices, all of them male.

If I recall, he had two attendants, one demon, the other human... Both were quite handsome in the game...

Half-awake, Aileen tries to draw on her game knowledge to work out what's happening.

"It isn't necessary for the demon king to save a mere human. What is this talk of a prince anyway? He has no need of a human rank."

"This man is the eldest prince of Imperial Ellmeyer. I haven't given up, you know. Someday, I'll have him marry a proper girl and build a loving family!"

"—Keith. How many times must I tell you that I intend to do no such thing?"

That's right; Keith is his human attendant. He's a childhood friend of the demon king, a young man with curly nut-brown hair, spectacles, and a mild demeanor. The demon king saved his life once when he was a child, and though his fellow humans persecute him for it, he serves Claude wholeheartedly.

"However, this young lady proposed to you, didn't she, Master Claude? The rumors about her aren't pleasant, but the fact that she's chosen you is admirable."

"Nothing else is, though. If you wish to keep the human woman as a pet, my king, I will make the necessary preparations, but..."

"There's no need for that, Beelzebuth."

Beelzebuth is his demon attendant. His long, perfectly straight hair and cold, porcelain beauty make him seem more like a devil than a monstrous demon. He is devoted to the demon king and will follow absolutely any order Claude gives him.

"It's all right, Master Claude. Even if her reputation's a touch less than ideal, the moment she set foot in this castle, her fate was decided. I will reshape her from the ground up and fashion her into a suitable bride for you."

"As I've been telling you, that won't be necessary, Keith."

"Then prepare to keep the human woman as a pet, my king."

"Why do you two insist on putting us together...?"

"Well, you are clearly not displeased, sire. Earlier, lightning struck because you were flustered."

As Beelzebuth speaks, Aileen hears someone choke. Keith nods.

"Yes, that's right. Your bouts of anger usually cause rather significant damage, what with all the earthquakes, volcanic eruptions, and the like. When you truly lose your temper, you even transform into a dragon... Don't leave me behind and fully become a demon, please."

Apparently, those were flustered lightning bolts, not wrathful ones. Aileen had assumed he'd been aiming at her with the intent to kill.

Feeling a little relieved, Aileen opens her eyes slightly. The sight that greets her is exactly what she expected, or rather, it's just like one of the scenes from the game.

Claude is seated in a magnificent chair, drinking tea, as his attendants offer their thoughts while standing on either side.

...This really is the game world, isn't it?

She's soared beyond surprise and now feels something closer to pure wonder. Of course, her survival is currently hanging in the balance, so she can't simply relax and be impressed.

"At any rate, I intend nothing of the sort, and neither does she. Look—she came with a sword. Perhaps she's come on someone's orders, or this may even be a trap of some kind. Either way, it will be a nuisance if she kills herself here."

"You misunderstand. I came of my own free will."

When she speaks, the game art moves. It's as if reality itself has sprung into motion.

All three of them direct different looks at Aileen, who is currently lying on the sofa. Keith's is concerned, while Beelzebuth's is overtly wary and hostile.

Claude's gaze, however, seems completely devoid of emotion.

"I brought the sword only for my self-defense. I intend you no harm."

"Do you have any illusions of defeating a demon with that toy, girl?"

Beelzebuth snorts. Aileen adjusts her position on the sofa, sitting up properly, and smiles back at him. Out of the corner of her eye, she also notes that the sword she brought is standing in the corner beside the sofa, its blade still naked.

"I would hate to die without putting up any resistance, you see."

"Resistance, hmm? Resistance is good. Very entertaining."

That patently demonic notion sends a shudder down her spine. However, she keeps it to herself and continues to hold her head high. Keith chides the other attendant.

"Enough of that. What meaning is there in terrorizing a young human girl? Dealing with the aftermath would be a headache. And on that note, young Lady d'Autriche…"

"Do call me Aileen, Master Keith."

"Hoh-hoh. You know of me?"

"I learned as much as I could about Master Claude before I came."

It would be more accurate to say she remembered, but she doesn't plan to tell them that much. Possibly because Claude isn't interested, he doesn't even blink.

In his demon form, as a dragon, he reigns over all creation. However, in his human form, he can't perfectly control his vast stores of magic, and his emotions cause abnormal phenomena. I already knew his character profile, and I was still caught by surprise.

Claude's anger leads to volcanic eruptions. His sorrow brings unending rain. When the demon king's heart is unsettled, it disturbs nature itself.

Demons are under the influence of his emotions as well. At the moment, demons don't attack humans because he has no inclination to attack them. If feelings of hatred or anger toward humanity drive him to awaken as the demon king, no doubt a great host of demons would immediately wreak havoc.

The moment Claude awakens, he'll transform into a dragon and cease to be human completely.

That's how he becomes the game's final boss, incidentally killing Aileen.

In other words, if Aileen doesn't want to die, she'll have to keep Claude from turning into the final boss.

Coming to that conclusion was a simple matter, but it presents a new problem.

For some reason, I can't remember the content of the "demon king's awakening" event...! There are quite a few other glaring holes in my memories, too! All I'm sure of is that he awakens just before the ending. I can't believe it! My life depends on this!

Thanks to her less-than-reliable recollections, Aileen has no idea what must be done to avert that critical event where Claude awakens as the demon king. It would have been fine if she could have at least managed to remember by now, but she couldn't bear to pin her hopes on something so uncertain when her life is on the line. And so she came up with another plan.

"Returning to the matter at hand, what brings you here, Miss Aileen? I'm told Prince Cedric called off your engagement, but if you're here to borrow the power of demons for your revenge, you've come to the wrong place. Master Claude's general policy is to spend his days in peace and quiet, you see."

"My, then I believe we shall get along. I am very fond of being safe as well."

"I hardly think people who value their safety would willingly come to see the demon king, let alone propose marriage."

"But if Master Claude will love me, I too will be able to spend my days in comforting repose."

She receives several looks of bewilderment, but she can't afford to care.

The one thing that allowed Claude to stay human and refrain from becoming the demon king was his love for Lilia.

However, Lilia can't romance Claude. Claude was one of those characters who could only be conquered on the second playthrough, and he wasn't unlocked until the player had seen the ending once. Unlike the game, reality only happens once. In other words, if he can't be romanced here and now, then he's almost certain to turn into the final boss.

In that case, Aileen will simply have to take Lilia's place and become the person who holds Claude back from the brink—by becoming the woman he loves.

Under the current circumstances, she decided that is the safest and most optimal plan available to her.

Aileen smiles at Claude.

"As such, please marry me. I'll make you happy."

"Is this human out of her mind?"

"I was just wondering that myself..."

"Beelzebuth, throw her out."

In response to Claude's curt order, Beelzebuth moves without hesitating. The moment she sees that, Aileen snatches up the sword that's leaning against the end of the sofa and holds it to her own neck.

"Bel, wait!"

Before Beelzebuth's hand reaches Aileen, he stops.

Seeing the events proceed exactly as she predicted, Aileen chuckles to herself. Had she been the heroine, she would have meekly allowed Beelzebuth to seize her and would have been forcibly returned home, gaining the rare and priceless experience of flying through the sky on her way. However, it isn't as if she has much of a choice in the matter, and avoiding the whole "getting flown home" event won't affect her relationship with Claude, so it shouldn't be an issue.

On the contrary, I need to play it up. If I'm *not the one he loves, it's pointless.*

Once he's stopped Beelzebuth, Claude frowns a little.

"What is the meaning of this?"

"If I must go home, I'll return on my own. I categorically

refuse to do anything as shameless as flying through the sky in the arms of a gentleman who is not my fiancé."

"Gentleman?"

Beelzebuth points at himself, looking perplexed. Claude, who's begun to rise from his chair, sits down again.

"I was only going to send you home in the usual way."

"No, Master Claude. Being carried by Beelzebuth and returning home by air is far removed from the ordinary. Her people would positively faint."

"...Very well. I'll take that into consideration, so put down the sword. I have little desire for such theatrics."

"You're a kind man."

Aileen lowers her sword as she flashes a smile at Claude, whose face is still expressionless. Keith puts a hand to his chin.

"Her reputation is...unflattering, but the young lady has spine. The d'Autriches are a great noble house, too. This chance may be too good to waste."

"Keith, enough idle talk... In any case, I refuse your request. Go home."

Still smiling, Aileen claps her hands together lightly.

"I'll take my leave if you agree to my proposal. Simple, isn't it?"

"As I said before, I don't understand what sense that makes. We've only just met. Why do you want to marry me? —Er..."

Although his expression doesn't change, Claude falters.

Aileen blinks. It feels as though a light breeze is blowing inside the room.

"Do you...love me?"

"Well, no."

When she answers his hesitant question with a blank look on her face, a strong gust of wind kicks up, also indoors. Keith hurries to soothe Claude.

"M–Master Claude, calm down! No whirlwinds, please!"

"Then what on earth is this about…?!"

"My king, I sympathize completely."

"I mean, we only just met."

"Yes, and that was the moment you decided to propose marriage! Besides, Cedric only just ended your engagement. What possessed you to do something so brazen right after—?"

The wind dies down immediately. It's probably because Aileen has pointed the sword directly at Master Claude's nose, which brought him to his senses.

Though there's a sword trained on their master, both Beelzebuth and Keith look unconcerned. That's only natural. If Claude got serious, he could turn Aileen to charcoal in an instant.

Even so, her pride compels her to speak.

"No doubt some of the fault lies with me. I admit that. However, are you saying I should simply accept my lot and spend the rest of my life weeping? Don't make me laugh. I have no intention of wasting another second on scum like him."

"…Scum? That's quite harsh."

"Yes. Women accrue love over time. I have decided that I will love you. Come, let us foster our affection."

"At swordpoint?"

Claude's eyes are cold, and Aileen directs her most beautiful smile at him.

"They say if you keep declaring that you are in love, it will eventually become truth. Shall we test that theory out?"

"I see."

Responding in a completely flat voice, Claude extends a hand. In spite of herself, Aileen hugs the sword to her chest. Gently, with his long fingers, he lifts a lock of hair that's fallen across her shoulder. He scrutinizes it suspiciously with his red eyes.

"In other words, you've come to seduce the demon king?"

"Sedu…"

Her cheeks flush. She's not accustomed to matters of love and men. In her previous life, *otome* games were her friends, and in this life, while she did have a fiancé, she had been raised as a sheltered noble lady, and tragically few moments of romance had actually passed between her and Cedric.

Nonetheless, she can't afford to show weakness by being flustered now. Still feeling timid, she forces herself to flaunt a brave smile at that lovely, expressionless face.

"Y-yes. I—I suppose that's what you'd call it."

"…Your voice seems to be trembling. Is that my imagination?"

"I-it most certainly is."

"You don't seem familiar enough with men to seduce one."

"Just who do you think I am? I am a veteran seductress! I could seduce a man before breakfast!!"

She's made that declaration firmly, but Claude's face is still empty. He only looks her over, examining her from the crown of her head to the tips of her toes.

Her makeup and clothes ought to be flawless, as always. Since she'd intended to venture to the demon king's castle, she didn't go all out, but she assures herself that her appearance is nothing a duke's daughter would need to be ashamed of. Still, for some reason, she suddenly feels embarrassed, and she stirs slightly.

H-having someone this gorgeous right in front of me makes me nervous… Oh, my hair! It's all mussed—

Belatedly, she notices: Her shoes are muddy. The lace on her dress apparently caught on something and frayed. On the whole, she's rather shabby. She charged straight through the woods, so it's only to be expected. Even so, this is a dire situation.

After all, in this era, being impeccably dressed is a woman's battle attire and her means of defense.

"I…I apologize for my unseemly appearance, especially when I've come to propose. I'll call again another day."

"There's no need."

Claude snaps his fingers. Aileen braces herself for a demon to appear, but a gentle breeze billows up from beneath her feet and swirls around her, scattering motes of light. The mud vanishes from her shoes, the frayed lace weaves itself back together, and the fabric that tore when it got caught on some branches is mended, then made clean again. Her disheveled hair is swept back by the wind as if it's being carefully combed out, and her fatigue lessens slightly.

…*It's magic.*

As Aileen blinks in surprise, Claude speaks to her brusquely.

"Now you won't need to come back. Go home."

"…I'll treasure this outfit."

"What?"

"I mean, it's an enchanted dress! That's marvelous!"

She twirls around, eyes sparkling, flaring out the dress she usually wears when she wants to travel unnoticed. At the same time, the bud of one of the flowers in a vase on the shelf opens. Is that magic as well? She watches the vase closely, her eyes shining, but that bud is the only one to open, and there are no further changes.

It seems strange, and Aileen turns to the expressionless Claude.

"Did that flower just bloom by magic as well?"

Claude doesn't answer. From behind him, off to the side, Keith gives a significant smile.

"The presence of a lady really does brighten the room, doesn't it? I'd worried that being surrounded by nothing but demons had warped your common sense and eye for beauty, Master Claude."

"Oh yes, that reminds me! Regarding those crows on the way here."

"...I keep telling you to go home. Are you hard of hearing?"

"I have heard you loud and clear. I'm simply refusing to go along. Now, about those crows—they are your servants, aren't they, Master Claude?"

Aileen draws herself up to her full height and stands firm as she faces down Claude, who's wearing an indefinable expression.

"It's all very well for them to warn those who enter the forest, but mocking visitors is in rather poor taste. The behavior of your vassals reflects on you, Master Claude. Do teach them to refrain from slander based on crude rumor."

"And why should I listen to anything you have to say?"

"Because it would be embarrassing for me to have a fiancé lacking in decorum."

"I don't recall becoming your fiancé."

"In addition, Master Beelzebuth, your attire is shameless. Utterly undignified."

Beelzebuth blinks in surprise, and Keith bursts out laughing, hugging his sides.

The only article of clothing Beelzebuth wears above the waist is a long vest. He shows a lot of skin and is dressed in the style of the East. When she saw his character design, she didn't think much of it, but by the customs of this country, intentionally exposing your skin is an outrageous thing to do. Moreover, it's midwinter. She feels cold just looking at him.

"I'll have something appropriate tailored for you. We'll also need to teach you proper etiquette."

"Wait, human girl. Why the hell would I do anything like that?"

"You are Master Claude's right-hand man, correct? Demon or not, you'll need to be proper enough to make public appearances."

"...Right-hand man, you say."

Beelzebuth's voice seems rather excited. He'll be easy to manipulate.

"As for you, Master Keith... You seem to have been making do with the same clothes for quite some time. Taking good care of your possessions is a fine thing, but we can't have you looking shabby in court. Do you have anything you can wear to social functions?"

"Oh, well, I had something tailored a few years ago. The thing is, Lady Aileen, and you won't believe it—while I'm technically a high official, I've sided too firmly with Master Claude, and so my wages are zero! Even though there are payments listed on the official books. Does that seem right to you?"

"Goodness."

Are his wages being embezzled? Aileen wonders as she frowns, falling deeper into thought.

"...I'm beginning to understand the situation. I take it Master Claude has no money, either?"

Abruptly, the flowers in the vase all drop their petals at once. When the two attendants notice this, they react swiftly.

"Master Claude, you don't have to let that trouble you. I enjoy life quite enough as it is."

"My king, if you desire money, I'll go steal some for you. Just say the word."

"Silence, both of you— Do you see now? There's no value in marrying me."

"Good heavens, don't worry about something so trivial. I'm quite reliable enough to provide for you, Master Claude. Why, if you'd like, I could even keep you in your demon form as a pet."

Instantly, lightning strikes just outside the window. At this point, Aileen isn't even startled. She simply laughs with an idle "My word."

Claude, whose face is still blank, groans.

"...What brought that on? Didn't you come here to seduce me?"

"That sort of thing suits me better."

Keep the final boss as a pet. Wouldn't that be a nice development? Aileen smiles, terribly pleased with the idea.

Claude looks back at her frostily.

"The fact that you don't understand that seduction would be preferable shows your sensibilities are questionable."

"I'll take that as a compliment... In any case, I hope you'll enter a contract by marrying me. With nothing more than your agreement, you will all be guaranteed lives of comfort and fortune."

"Wow, she sounds like a new type of missionary."

"Master Claude. All I ask in return is your love. Thanks to a certain piece of human scum, I've been shown just how demanding a request that is."

Claude looks up. While it's faint, there seems to be some emotion in his face now.

Thinking that if she can only make him agree, she's won, Aileen presses him.

"You are a kind man. Surely, you do not hate humans whole-heartedly. As a result, the demons feel rather stifled, which in turn pains you. Am I wrong?"

"……"

"Personally, I hope those who wronged me get devoured by demons. However, if you wished for that, it would actually happen. How heavy that responsibility must be, and how conflicted you must feel—and yet here you are, resisting that very temptation. I respect your strength."

For the first time, Claude's confusion shows in his face. He widens his eyes. In them, Aileen's reflection wears a devilish smile.

"If you marry me, I will protect both you and the demons you cherish. I won't make you bear that burden alone. I may not look it, but I would have been empress one day. I do understand these things."

Abruptly, Claude's face goes blank again. It's as if he's snuffed out his emotions.

Aileen blinks, and then his lovely face is right in front of her.

"Enough. Leave."

They aren't words, but a spell.

He taps her on the forehead with his index finger; she totters, her body rises lightly—and in the next moment, her knees buckle, dropping her onto something soft.

She's sitting on her bed. Her bedroom has abruptly materialized around her, and she blinks at it repeatedly, feeling bitter regret. He's forcibly magicked her back home.

"…He pulled one over me. Was I close to convincing him…? Or did I make a mistake somewhere?"

Claude's reactions were hard to pin down. She'd thought he seemed detached at first, but then he'd been clearly agitated for a moment, only to quickly regain his calm. Through all that, he didn't smile even once.

Squinting at the morning sun that lances through the gap in her white curtains, Aileen broods.

Perhaps I shouldn't have made it sound quite so much like a threat. I guess it's true that no heroine would have talked that way... However, if I'm not misremembering, being teleported away was something that only happened after he'd become quite fond of you.

When Claude, frightened by his growing attraction to the heroine, decided to put some distance between them, he'd use teleportation to make it happen physically.

Aileen wonders if it's safe to deduce from his actions that this went rather well for their first meeting.

"I do still have time. Starting tomorrow, perhaps I should try being less aggressive? I'll refine my approach as well..."

"Your pardon, Miss Aileen. Miss Aileen... Are you awake?"

Aileen calls to the maid who's knocked on her bedroom door.

"I am. What is it?"

"The master says he'd like to speak with you. He says it is high time to get back on your feet already."

Come to think of it, she was supposed to have retired to her room from the shock of her broken engagement.

Are you serious, Father? It's only been a day. He's the same as ever...

When she was only Aileen and didn't remember her past life, his behavior seemed normal to her, but now it feels rather harsh. Ordinarily, if it hadn't been for the shock of regaining the memories from her past life, she wouldn't have been able to recover so quickly.

However, there's no helping some things in life. Sighing, Aileen gets up from the bed and opens her bedroom door.

"All right. I do hope I haven't caused him trouble of any sort."

"The master's the same as always. However, it does look as though the broken engagement with Prince Cedric has caused some difficulties... I believe that may be what he wants to discuss."

"I see."

Aileen responds shortly as she gathers herself. *In that case, I've earned the lecture.*

"Let's get this unpleasantness out of the way quickly. Let me get ready and then— Actually, no."

Glancing at her enchanted clothes, Aileen shakes her head. The maid looks perplexed.

"I'll go as I am. Bring my breakfast up later, if you would."

The remnants of the spell have become a faint breeze that flows past his feet.

Dropping heavily into a chair, Claude closes his eyes, pressing his fingers to his temples.

"What in blazes was that woman?"

"Oh, you sent her away by force? Don't tell me you left her somewhere preposterous."

"Of course not. I did as I should and sent her to her own room."

Behind his eyelids, he watches the young woman who vanished before him fall onto her bed. He can see her muttering something to herself, but he avoids listening. Clairvoyance is handy, but picking up sound puts more strain on him, and more than anything, he's aware that eavesdropping with it is unconscionable.

Claude opens his eyes. The first thing he sees is Keith pouring him a fresh cup of tea.

"I certainly hope so. Good grief, things have been lively since last night, haven't they?"

"You didn't have to send her back her personally, my king. I would have flung her out the window toward her mansion for you."

"That would have killed her, you know."

"You could kill that woman, and she still wouldn't die."

Beelzebuth makes that declaration with a straight face, drawing a droll smile out of Keith.

Claude can't claim to disagree.

"I suspect she'll be back soon. What should we do, my king?"

"Ignore her until she gets tired of it."

"I get the feeling you'll make a decision one way or another before the young lady tires of this, Master Claude..."

"Sire, sire! News! The emperor's messenger comes!"

A jet-black crow is out on the terrace, cawing and flapping their wings. *Well, well.* Keith smiles.

"We're getting so many callers today."

"Tell the demons to come inside the gate. I'll put up a barrier."

At Claude's command, the crow promptly takes to the air, flying away. As he watches them go, Beelzebuth steps forward.

"My king. If you intend to run them off, I'll go."

"You mustn't do that. Remember the nonaggression pact. If you and your kind get violent, even if it's for the demon king's sake, it'll mean endless trouble again."

Keith rebukes him mockingly, and Beelzebuth clicks his tongue in irritation.

"Humans truly are all imbeciles. We won't do a thing to them unless the king orders it."

"Come to think of it, Master Claude, why did you let Miss Aileen into the castle?"

"Because she came to see me herself."

Given the circumstances, he'd thought the least he could do was hear what she had to say. That was all.

Although, it turned out to be nonsense. Oh, but...

"I respect your strength."

No. Don't let your guard down. Not unless you want to finally become a demon.

Closing his eyes again, he focuses on expanding his awareness, widening its range to the palisade that encircles his castle and the surrounding forest.

No one will reach the castle. He won't allow it.

After all, this is the castle of the demon king.

Rudolph Lauren d'Autriche is famous as the shrewdest prime minister in the Ellmeyer Empire's history. However, at a glance, almost no one would have guessed it.

At their first meetings, everyone who saw him would undoubtedly say, *"What, that mild, unreliable-looking fellow?"*

"Ah, Aileen. I'm glad you're here. I'm sorry to ask for you so early; this was the only moment I could spare."

Smiling, her father beckons her to enter his study. Aileen sits down on the reception sofa in front of his ebony desk and waits for her father to take his seat opposite her.

"It's too bad about Prince Cedric."

"I'm very sorry, Father."

Her engagement to Cedric had been a marriage of convenience—a maneuver that influenced political negotiations. It had been an important move, intended to further solidify the standing of the d'Autriche duchy. Not only that, but since her father is the prime minister, the scandal over the broken engagement is probably also affecting his work as well.

Setting aside the question of whether it will impact this father of mine...

"There's nothing to be done. After all, you've clearly drifted from Prince Cedric's preferences."

As he tells her this, looking sad, Aileen's expression turns serious. She apologizes one more time.

"...I really am terribly sorry."

"Even so, I did hope it might stick on the strength of the d'Autriche name. I tell you, the love of young people is a force. You yourself always said, 'Prince Cedric understands me, so it's all right.'"

"I'm really, truly, terribly sorry."

"I actually thought that you would more inconsolable. I heard you'd withdrawn to your room."

Her father sighs.

"And yet you look happier than I expected. That's rather disappointing..."

There's genuine regret in his voice, and Aileen's cheeks tense up.

There it is! He's such a sadist! His daughter's engagement was broken, and he's still…!

Her kind father has an extremely troublesome predilection for taking delight in watching the misfortunes of others. Family is no exception. In fact, since he lovingly doesn't hide it from his family members, it's worse for them.

If she told him there was a problem she didn't understand, he'd cheerfully sit there and watch her struggle. If she was chagrined over having lost at something, he'd enjoy analyzing the various reasons for her defeat. Thanks to that, Aileen has grown so resilient that ordinary insults and setbacks don't so much as faze her, but she's developed a terribly unendearing personality that prefers searching for solutions over crying, and fighting rather than getting depressed.

Put that way, she starts to think it may very well be her father's fault that Cedric jilted her.

"And here I was so looking forward, every single day, to the moment when he would ultimately spurn you."

"…So there was no doubt in your mind that one day I would be spurned."

"He turned you down so miserably that it nearly beggared belief… Oh, my poor Aileen… In your tear-soaked grief, you would surely have been the most adorable creature alive, and yet…!"

"You were having a grand old time by fantasizing about that, weren't you?"

"But now look at you: You seem practically cheerful. The servants stopped me earlier, so I gave up, but…I knew I should have charged into your room."

Giving silent thanks to the outstanding servants, Aileen answers as calmly as she can.

"I've resolved to forget Master Cedric entirely."

"I see. Well, that's good. I never dreamed he was that much of a fool."

Smiling faintly, Rudolph summarily purges the prince from his mind. His utter lack of hesitation makes even his daughter shudder.

"Still, Aileen. That doesn't restore your position, nor does it mend the family's wounded honor."

"...I'm aware of that, Father. I regret bringing shame on the house of d'Autriche."

"On to the main topic, then."

Smiling, her father laces his fingers together. Merrily.

In other words, Aileen isn't going to like what's coming next. She sits up straighter.

"You were preparing to launch a business, weren't you? As I recall, you had made arrangements for the development and sale of medicines, plus plans for transportation and road improvements, so that you could better find a market for them."

"? Yes. My brothers told me that I could secure the raw materials by having them produced on d'Autriche lands and that I should develop a distribution route to increase profits."

The d'Autriche duchy is vast and fertile. However, that abundance is only true when looking at the territory as a whole, and since the duchy is so large, there are regional disparities. Her brothers are of a mind that areas that are not prosperous—in other words, sprawling rural tracts that often contain nothing but dirt—should be developed and improved. They devised various uses for the plants that naturally grow in those areas and are working hard to raise the living standard of the inhabitants by setting up the production of specialty products in those districts. They let Aileen participate in that work.

The daughter of a duke, one who was the crown prince's fiancée at that, was personally conducting business and trade. Naturally, there had been criticism. However, they silenced the critics by arguing that the development of medicines would be of great benefit to the masses. They also anticipated turning a tidy profit by popularizing items that were more accessible—such as soaps, salves, and disinfectants—among the townspeople before they began dealing in pharmaceuticals, which were more difficult to handle.

As a matter of fact, the finances of Ellmeyer's imperial family aren't as solid as one might assume. *That was why I wanted to at least bring a vast dowry with me when I married Cedric, for his sake*— After letting her mind wander that far, she tugs her thoughts back to the present.

"I also recall receiving your approval for that, Father. What about it?"

"It's all going to Prince Cedric. You could say it's becoming a public enterprise."

"Huh…?"

Aileen is stunned. Smiling sardonically, Rudolph goes on.

"When you established the trading company, it was in both your own name and Prince Cedric's, wasn't it? The ability to produce medicine is the ability to produce poison, too. If the court tells us it should be under state control, we can't very well argue, can we?"

She arranged plans for distribution, prepared everything from trade routes to formulas for medicines, and the medical trials have already produced excellent results. In other words...

"He's just taking the profits?!"

Aileen sounds aghast, and it makes Rudolph smile cheerfully.

"It sounds as though Lady Lilia advised him that he mustn't leave all the responsibility to you. Apparently, Prince Cedric worked up some enthusiasm for it. By dabbling in commerce, he may acquire a feel for the flow of money and the common man's perspective all at the same time. That would be a fine thing, wouldn't it?"

"No, no, no, no, that's just stealing!! He's only taking the best parts!!"

"This was your fault, Aileen."

He says the words mildly, but Aileen gasps and falls silent. Her father's eyes aren't smiling.

"Ordinarily, a unilaterally broken engagement is worthy of criticism, even if the other party is a member of the imperial family. However, given the current circumstances, our peers deem it only natural for the prince to break off the engagement. Consequently, we have been awarded no compensation for damages, and they've taken the capital we invested in the business as well."

"I—I apologize for my incompetence...!"

"Just like your mother, you have no eye for men, and on top of that, although you're adorable, you have no talent for courtship."

His tone isn't critical at all; he's merely pointing out the facts, and it leaves her at a loss for words.

As Aileen writhes in agony, Rudolph smiles happily at her. She knows it's a sign of his love, but she wishes he'd show a little self-restraint.

"Not only that, but…"

"There's more?"

"Why yes, indeed there is."

Half glaring at him, she watches as her father extracts a single letter from a stack that's being held down by a paperweight. Its seal has already been broken.

"We received an invitation yesterday. It's for a soiree, two months from now."

"A soiree? For me? …Now?"

Soirees are group marriage interviews, places to look for a future spouse. As someone whose engagement has just been broken, the normal thing would have been for Aileen to refrain from them for a time, while the hosts, reluctant to associate with a girl whose reputation is scandalous, would naturally stop inviting her.

"And what tactless fool sent this invitation?"

"It's from Prince Cedric and Lady Lilia."

She feels dizzy.

"Oh, there's a letter in there, too. Written by Lady Lilia herself. She says it's a secret, but they'll be announcing their engagement at the event as well, so she would like for you to attend. I've also been summoned. She's really something, this Lady Lilia."

"Yes, she truly is… I'd like to learn from her example…"

"It sounds as though Prince Cedric is going to unveil a new policy at this soiree, based on the business he took over from you. At the same time, he's ordered you to sign a written dissolution of your engagement in front of the assembly."

In other words, she's supposed to discarded by Cedric in public again. It would have been perfectly doable to sign a written dissolution of the engagement in private. He's going out of his way to make it a public event.

He really wants to take me down a peg or two, doesn't he? Or does he genuinely think it's the correct thing to do, since they're the victims? The possibility is so high that she can't even bring herself to laugh.

"He also wants you to sign an agreement transferring control of your part of the business. By showing humility in public, you'll apparently take the edge off your bad reputation. According to him, it's an act of mercy."

Suppressing all her emotions currently bubbling up, Aileen exhales heavily.

"In other words, if I don't attend, I'll have rejected Prince Cedric's mercy, and if I do attend, he'll take over my business, and my engagement will be broken in public again. Either way, I'll be a fine laughingstock."

"Well? What will you do?"

Normally, refusing would be her only choice. As long as she sent her signature, the formalities could proceed without trouble, and no time would be wasted. If instead of attending she made a display of her grief, she might be able to attract sympathy from those around her— All that being said...

"I'll attend. When someone picks a fight with me, I accept the challenge and send it right back, with interest."

No point in being meek now, not after speaking so sharply earlier. Aileen smiles. *Forget the sympathy; I'll go in swinging.* Rudolph nods, looking satisfied.

"Very good. You're a daughter of the house of d'Autriche, all right. If you'd tucked tail and ran after they made such a fool out of you, I would've disowned you and tossed you into the seedier side of town or somewhere like that."

Her father might actually do it while pretending to weep. As she responds, her cheeks tense.

"They may speak ill of you as well, Father. There will be whispers that say you're lacking in common sense."

"That's fine. I'll listen to the many spiteful comments about you, then nod away as I apologize and mentally add their names to my list."

"I won't ask what kind of list that is, but as long as you don't mind, Father, then I suppose…"

"In that case, make sure you earn enough by the time the soiree is held to recoup the losses the house of d'Autriche has sustained."

He speaks as if it's nothing, and Aileen frowns.

"Please don't casually hoist outrageous demands upon me. By 'recoup,' are you telling me to start a brand-new enterprise? I'm not as brilliant as my brothers, Father. Moreover, in a scant two months?"

"Figure it out yourself. A failed would-be empress who allows her reputation to remain in the mud is no daughter of mine."

Her father smiles. His eyes are dead serious.

A sudden chill runs down Aileen's spine. If she opts not to attend the soiree and fails to restore her honor and the honor of the family, her father might genuinely abandon her.

Cedric is the crown prince, meaning Aileen has fallen out of favor with an individual who will someday be emperor. If she doesn't rally somehow, she'll simply become a burden on the house of d'Autriche eventually. A daughter with a ruined reputation.

If I recall, there was a game event that had me losing all my rank and status…although I only remember it vaguely…

She finds some comfort in her hunch that she may have avoided tripping some sort of unfortunate flag just now. Besides, it isn't as if there's no way to fulfill her father's demand. At this point, the power of the d'Autriche duchy is still hers to use.

In any case, she'll need money if she's going to care for the demon king.

There's also the matter of Master Claude... I did sense some potential there. Where there's a will, there's a way.

She's steeled herself. As a result, she feels as if she'll sleep well tonight.

Later, in the dead of night, Aileen bolts up with a shriek.

"Attending the soiree was the trigger for being evicted! What is this?! Why do these memories always come back too late?! Is it divine harassment?!"

Aileen howls at the pitch-black ceiling, but of course, no kind god answers her.

✦ Second Act ✦
The Villainess Is Not Cute, and So She Does Not Cry

In the interval between the broken engagement and the ending, there were two major events that were related to Aileen's fate. One was the "demon king's awakening" event, which led directly to her own demise.

The other was the soiree event, at which Cedric publicly announced the dissolution of his engagement to Aileen and his new engagement to Lilia.

Aileen, the villainous young noblewoman, refused to accept the broken engagement. In an attempt to prevent the announcement of Lilia and Cedric's betrothal, she hired some ne'er-do-wells and plotted to have Lilia kidnapped so that she wouldn't be able to attend the soiree. However, the plot was ultimately foiled in advance by a pseudo–love interest (which was how Marcus looked to Aileen).

Unaware of this and intent on winning Cedric back, Aileen attended the soiree, only for Lilia to appear and accuse her, causing her to be disowned from the d'Autriche family, stripped of her rank, and thrown into the streets. This is a development Aileen would dearly love to avoid.

After all, she doesn't have the sort of abilities that would let her survive as a commoner. Unfortunately, her past self didn't have them, either.

That said, not attending the soiree is no longer an option.

This morning, when she'd tested her father by saying, "*Perhaps I won't attend that soiree after all,*" he looked startled and asked, "*Do you want to lose your rank?*" He meant every word. Her father would definitely follow through and disown her. Failing to attend would yield the same results.

That said, trying to prevent a kidnapping incident that some-one else might perpetrate would involve getting close to Lilia, which would ironically look very much like a kidnapping attempt. No doubt she'd seem far too suspicious.

In short, as things stand, she has no concrete way to avoid triggering the event.

However, at the very least, I must take Master Claude to the soiree as my partner and make it obvious to everyone that I'm genuinely happy about the broken engagement…!

If she can do that much, then even if someone else kidnaps Lilia, Aileen won't be immediately implicated. Since there's no telling what may happen, she needs to make the moves she's sure she can make.

She also has to fulfill her father's request and "recoup the losses."

There's no time— I'll just have to work on both in tandem.

And so even though it's been only a day, Aileen is walking down a familiar path through the forest. She's wearing a tidy white dress and lace-up boots, carrying a rather large basket, and twirling a parasol. Even she feels she's the very picture of a perfect young noblewoman.

The trouble is that she's been walking in circles for just about an hour.

"Could this be the barrier, perhaps?"

Untying the handkerchief she attached to a tree branch to mark her path earlier, Aileen closes her parasol.

She looks up at the sky but doesn't see a single shape in it. The dense canopy also seems somehow artificial.

"It was the same as the last time until the palisade just before the forest, and yet... Isn't anyone here?"

She looks around. The only response is unnaturally deep silence.

As an experiment, she calls again.

"To think he's too frightened to show himself to me! The demon king seems to be quite the coward."

Nothing in the scenery changes. However, she feels a presence of sorts. They must be angry that she's insulted the demon king.

Am I the only one who can't see any of them? It was like this in the game, too; the demons really are fond of him.

It's likely that Claude has a soft spot for the demons as well.

Aileen gives a modest sigh.

"All right. I'll give up on seeing him today. However, someone *is* there, correct? Won't you come out? I've brought a present, as an apology."

There's no response. However, vaguely, she senses that her watchers are bewildered.

Aileen opens the lid of her basket, displaying its contents to the empty space. There are a large quantity of cookies in various flavors, like almond and chocolate.

Thanks to the game, she knows that—surprisingly—demons are partial to human food.

"I made them myself. I don't know whether they'll suit your

tastes, but I hope you'll help yourselves to them. And also, I meant to give this to one of the crows."

She takes a small bow tie out of the basket's inner pocket. The silk ribbon is deep crimson, very smooth, and definitely not cheap.

Ribbon in hand, Aileen smiles.

"I said as much yesterday, but the way the crows welcome guests reflects on the demon king. As such, I'd like all the demons to be dignified as well."

There are no visible changes in the scenery. Even so, the bemused atmosphere is palpable.

"Hence, this accessory. Do you suppose the strongest of the crows, your leader, could wear it? It will serve as a mark of the demon king's trusted gatekeeper."

There is no answer. However, she feels as if she's heard a voice say, *Mark of the gatekeeper.*

It's the same buoyant tone she heard from Beelzebuth yesterday in response to her saying "*right-hand man.*"

"Will no one come forth as a representative? Or has the demon king forbidden that as well?"

"Human girl, hand it over!"

With a sudden rustle of wings, a crow flies out of empty space. They're somewhat larger than the rest. With eyes the same red color as the demon king's, this one has gone out of their way to carry a skull in their talons, which are far larger and sharper than would ordinarily be possible. That can't be what passes for fashion among demons, can it?

Once the crow has landed on the ground, Aileen kneels to put herself on eye level with them.

"You are the strongest?"

"That's right! The demon king's gatekeeper! Girl, give me the proof!"

"I'll put it on you, so turn the other way, would you? Your eyes are the same color as the demon king's, I see."

"Same as the demon king!"

The crow seems perfectly giddy. They spin around, turning their back to her. Aileen sets the open basket down right in front of them.

"If you'd like, you may sample any cookie that strikes your fancy."

"You have a good attitude, girl. Almond for me!"

Dexterously picking up a single almond cookie with the tip of their beak, they crunch into it. In the meantime, Aileen gently wraps the bow tie around their neck.

Their down is fluffier than she expected, and quite pleasant.

"Yum! Yum! Girl, you bring good offerings! I'll allow it."

"My, how kind of you. You have lovely feathers, don't you?"

"Because I'm the strongest! Girl, you have good eyes—Ghk!"

The crow flinches. A shudder runs through them, and then they flop over onto their side. The next moment, her vision opens up.

In a twinkling, the bright track through the woods is transformed into the demon king's gloomy forest. A murder of crows sits in the tops of the dead trees, just like yesterday. There are demons who resemble rats and moles, too. She's been completely surrounded.

However, Aileen picks up the crow, who is still trembling all the way to the tips of their feathers. Holding them firmly, she puts the tip of the knife concealed in the end of her parasol to them and gives an elegant smile.

"Everyone stay where you are, please. What a foolish demon. To think, trusting a human!"

"**What decent human would say that?!**"

"**Ghk... What...did you do, girl...?!**"

"I laced the cookie with a numbing agent."

"**Die! I'll kill you, girl!**"

"Dear me, do you wish to cause trouble for the demon king? I belong to the house of d'Autriche. If I am killed by demons, it will worsen his position."

Aileen smiles thinly. The crows caw at her raucously, as if they're condemning her. The other demons look downright murderous as well. Apparently worried for the companion in her clutches, however, they don't attack.

Paying them no heed, she raises her voice.

"Now then, Master Claude, if you wish to save this demon, present yourself! If you don't, I'll pluck its feathers one by one until it's bald—"

She's interrupted by a blast of wind. Hair as black as darkness. Crimson eyes that gleam with a richer color than jewels glare down at her from midair.

"**Sire!**"

"**Demon king! The human girl betrayed us!**"

The demon king lightly descends to the ground, and the demons cling to him. Aileen beams.

"Good day to you, Master Claude."

His only response is silence. She's managed to draw out the person she was after, though, and that's enough.

"Would you heal this demon? It should recover naturally with time, but..."

Claude kneels in front of her. Then, gently, he touches the paralyzed crow in her arms.

The next instant, the crow's eyes fly open, and they begin flapping their wings. Apparently, the numbness is already gone.

"I'd expect no less of you."

Aileen is impressed. The crow, who has struggled free of her arms, lands on Claude's shoulder and shrieks at her.

"You're dead, girl! I'll kill you, I swear!"

"Oh, but we're even now, aren't we?"

"How so?"

Rising to his feet, Claude directs that brief question at her. Aileen smiles at him.

"I haven't forgotten, you know. The way the crows surrounded me and heaped abuse on me."

Although Claude's expression has been as cold as ice, faint uncertainty flickers through it. Dusting herself off, Aileen moves to stand directly in front of him.

"If that makes you feel beholden to me, train your crows properly in the first place. Isn't that right, little crow I just deceived?"

"Kill!"

"Let's make up. As an apology, I'll give you a chocolate cookie."

"You can't fool me! No more fooling me!"

"It's all right. Only the almond kind have the numbing agent mixed into them. As proof, you can watch me eat half."

Aileen takes out a chocolate cookie, then bites into it with a light crunch. The crow with the bow tie stares at her until she's swallowed.

"You see? It's all right. Come, now. Let's be friends again, shall we?"

She holds out the half-eaten cookie. They glare with their red eyes from Aileen to Claude and back. With a sigh, Claude takes the cookie from Aileen, then has a bite.

Aileen wasn't expecting this development, and she blinks. His expression cool, Claude swallows, then offers the remaining morsel to the demon on his shoulder.

"It's fine to eat."

Immediately, the crow latches onto the cookie.

"Yum! Chocolate is good!"

"D-demon king..."

The surrounding demons begin to stir restlessly. Claude looks at Aileen.

"Everything but the almond kind is safe, you said?"

"Y-yes... But whatever shall I do? This really isn't the place for..."

"...What do you mean? Don't tell me you did something to the chocolate cookies as well."

"Yes. I'd hoped to put you in the mood, Master Claude, so I added an aphrodisiac that only affects men."

As Aileen responds brightly, lightning strikes behind her.

"There's something wrong with you."

Claude looks haggard. Aileen tilts her head dubiously.

"Do you think so? I'd based that plan on the assumption that you had a strong sense of responsibility, Master Claude."

"Responsibility for what?"

"Gracious, you'd actually make me say it?"

"Ahhh-ha-ha-ha-ha-ha, ah-ha-ha-ha-ha-ha!"

Keith, who's served them black tea, abruptly bursts out laughing as if he just can't take it anymore. Claude glares at him.

"What exactly is funny about this, Keith?"

"W-well, I mean, a young lady who'd take a demon hostage, threaten the demon king, then dose him with a love-potion? That's quite a gift she's got."

"You flatter me, Master Keith."

She takes a sip of the tea he's prepared for her, then sets the cup down on its saucer.

They're currently in the parlor where Aileen awakened the previous day. Claude insisted that she go home at first, but she adamantly refused, and they've finally reached a compromise, leading to the current sit-down.

The fact that this is the only room they can host guests is problematic, but the tea she's been given is good, and the sofa she's seated in is quite comfortable. Keith, who's convulsing with laughter, must have arranged for them.

"It is a pity, though. To think that aphrodisiacs don't affect Master Claude..."

"As if such an insolent scheme would work on the king!"

Beelzebuth sounds oddly proud. Smiling wryly, Keith supplements his answer.

"There have been all sorts of attempts to poison Master Claude. He's built up a tolerance, and potions tend not to work on him. And to be frank, he's the demon king, after all."

"My. In that case, even if I used a stronger dose, it wouldn't work?"

"I will never eat anything you bring me again."

"Then I'll think up some other method."

"You don't have to."

"But I'm running out of time."

Putting a hand to her cheek, Aileen gives an anxious sigh.

"Are you going to inquire about my reasons?"

"I don't want to know."

"Duly noted. The truth is, I'll be attending a soiree in two months' time…"

"Was that preamble about whether I was going to ask really necessary?"

"…And I would truly love to have you attend as my escort, Master Claude."

"So knowing is mandatory. I see… But why would that require an aphrodisiac?"

"? If I'd simply asked you, would you have agreed?"

When she asks him that, her eyes round, Claude's face goes blank. Keith bursts out laughing, holding his sides.

"S-so you thought you'd establish a fait accompli first. Oh yes, I see…"

"You 'see.' Ha! Girl! If you wish to attract the king's attention, then strip naked and demonstrate your intent to submit. His Majesty is kind. I'm sure he will take pity on you."

Claude, who is seated in an armchair, freezes up, but Beelzebuth's eyes are serious.

For just a moment, Aileen's expression turns sober. However, she promptly recovers her smile, then places a hand over her chest.

"If that is what you wish, Master Claude."

"It isn't. Be silent, Bel. And you! Don't you dare disrobe…!"

"Then will you attend the soiree with me?"

Claude holds his head. Keith speaks up; he's laughed so much that he's wheezing.

"A-a soiree... Well, really, why not? I'll do my very best to help you get ready!"

"My! Thank you very much, Master Keith."

"Wait. Don't act as if the matter's been settled. I haven't said I'm going."

"We will not allow you to force something the king does not want on him, humans."

Beelzebuth takes a step forward, as if to shield Claude.

"A human soiree? I'll destroy the whole pointless thing, venue and all."

"Master Beelzebuth. You don't understand in the slightest."

"What?!"

"Bel. She's going to trap you. I can see it coming. Don't."

"Don't you want to show the world Master Claude's splendor?"

Beelzebuth's eyes widen just as she predicted. Claude puts a hand to his face. Watching him out of the corner of her eye, Aileen smoothly continues her negotiation.

"Master Claude is splendid, is he not?"

"...Of course, the king is magnificent."

"Then he simply must attend the soiree. He cannot truly be an object of awe unless he reveals himself to the humans. Your demon king will shine."

"The king will...shine..."

Beelzebuth darts a surreptitious glance at Claude, torn. If the king his people love and respect were to be venerated and revered by all, of course he'd be happy about it.

Consequently, Claude can't casually dash the demons' hopes.

"Will you escort me, Master Claude?"

"...In the first place, I am the demon king. I would never be able to attend in the normal way. Someone is bound to interfere before I reach the venue. It's tiresome."

"Master Claude... Did you not hear what I said yesterday? I distinctly remember telling you that I would be keeping you like a pet."

Keith cracks up yet again, while Claude's expression goes beyond a grimace and reverts to a blank slate.

"I had decided to ignore it."

"Then let me tell you once more. You will be mine. In other words, you are the fiancé of the daughter of the house of d'Autriche."

"...To begin with, let me point out that the 'fiancé' premise is incorrect."

"What I am saying is that I will be with you. You may simply walk straight in, boldly, through the main entrance. What does it matter if you are the demon king? I will bear all responsibility."

As Aileen confidently volunteers, Claude watches her with an indescribable expression.

"Do you have any other concerns?"

When she arbitrarily moves the conversation along, Claude recrosses his legs, looking away slightly.

"...You will damage your position. If the court thinks you are consorting with demons..."

"My... My, oh my, oh *my*! Are you worried for me, Master Claude?!"

Clasping her hands in front of her bosom, Aileen leans in closer until she's right in his face. Startled, Claude draws back, but unfortunately for him, he's still sitting down, so the distance between them doesn't change.

"Have no fear. At the moment, my reputation couldn't be

worse. People can't possibly hate me more or give me a wider berth than they're already doing, so there's no need to worry!"

"Who says that about themselves so confidently?"

"You see, in any case, this soiree is being held to mock me. I must publicly consent to having my engagement broken, humbly hand over complete control of the trading company I established, and congratulate Prince Cedric and Lady Lilia on their betrothal. In doing so, I'll supposedly earn Prince Cedric's forgiveness. Personally, I'm still not convinced whether my behavior was so bad that it merits all that penance."

She gives a smile that doesn't go past her lips. Claude responds with silence. Beelzebuth snorts.

"Everything humans do is truly petty."

"And that is where Master Claude comes in, Master Beelzebuth!"

When Aileen abruptly calls his name, Beelzebuth twitches and pulls away slightly.

"A man who will give people no choice but to fall silent, even if he is standing by my side as I am now! Who but Master Claude is so perfect in appearance, title, and every other way?"

"I... I see...!"

"Don't give me that— Enough of this. I will not attend."

At his unexpectedly firm tone, Aileen falls silent. Although Beelzebuth has been muttering to himself and Keith has continued laughing uncontrollably, they've both gone quiet in the next moment.

Claude rises from his armchair without a sound, his eyes fixed on Aileen.

"Miss d'Autriche. I must ask you to leave. I won't see you off. Walk home, on your own."

"...And if I refuse?"

"Do as you please. You bring me nothing but trouble, and I'll have nothing to do with you from now on."

Claude turns on his heel. Inwardly, Aileen feels keen regret.

So the support of the house of d'Autriche would be "nothing but trouble." I expect that's what he means.

True, Claude probably doesn't need the authority nor financial clout of the d'Autriche duchy. After all, he is the demon king. He can get anything he wants, if he ever feels like it. The fact that he hasn't only means he doesn't want to.

Then what does *he want? In the game, I seem to recall that he was drawn to Lilia because she treated him like an ordinary human. However, Lilia was the Maid of the Sacred Sword and completely incompatible with demons, so...*

How did their relationship form in the game? Come to think of it, she still hasn't remembered yet.

—And that's when it happens.

"Demon king! Demon king! A lost child!"

Although Claude is already halfway out of the room, the voice that darts in from the terrace stops him. As he turns, the terrace door opens, and a crow with a bow tie flies in.

However, the moment they see Aileen, they look frightened.

"Geh! You're still here...!"

"Gracious. Mind your tongue, Almond."

"What?! I'm not an almond!"

"It's your name. More accurately, it's *Crow That Ate the Almond Cookie and Got Paralyzed*."

They fix her with an angry glare. However, Claude steps past Aileen and holds out a hand.

"Never mind her. What happened?"

"No sign of coming back! A young fenrir has left the forest!"

"After venturing beyond the barrier?"

On hearing Claude's murmur, Aileen turns to Keith.

"'Left the forest,' as in the forest surrounding this castle?"

"That's right. Remember how there's a palisade before you get into the woods? Master Claude casts a barrier along that and watches whenever humans enter or leave. To protect the demons from the humans, you see."

"In order to ensure the nonaggression pact is thoroughly observed...?"

"You're Prime Minister d'Autriche's daughter, all right. So you knew about it?"

When Claude was banished to the abandoned castle, he exchanged a pledge with the emperor.

He would not allow the demons to attack humans. In exchange, humans would not attack the demons. By concluding that treaty and agreeing to surrender his right to inherit the throne, Claude secured a land of peace in the form of this castle and the forest surrounding it.

At only ten years of age, he had successfully negotiated a treaty with the emperor. That alone was enough to show that he was an intelligent individual.

...But was that truly what you wanted?

Aileen can't bring herself to think that things can be splendid if they require sacrifice to gain.

Life is splendid when one wins absolutely everything.

"So the young fenrir went in the direction of the eastern second layer, hmm?"

"The eastern second layer— Isn't that where the Holy Knights' training ground and the academy are located?"

Alucato, the imperial capital, spreads out like a fan with

the royal castle at its focal point and is divided into five layers. Generally speaking, the first layer is a residential district where the nobility lives, while the second holds government offices, banks, and other public facilities. The third is the commercial district, and the fourth is a residential district for the common people. The fifth holds everything else, including the slums, where the very poorest live. The red-light district is there, and public safety is bad—in any case, that's the general layout.

This abandoned castle and its forest are located behind the royal castle, and they fit together with the fan shape to make a complete circle. The walls and gates between the layers don't block the forest, so it's possible to enter or leave it from the ends of any layer. Depending on the place, there might be palisades or walls nominally barring the way, and there are signs that warn against entering the forest, but there are also brooks and geographical issues that make it impossible to completely seal all the ways into the forest.

"What a place to go... The residents of the fifth layer would overlook a young demon as long as there were no notable incidents, but that's a tricky spot, and the people of the second layer are bound to make a fuss about this."

"Can't Master Claude just whisk it home by magic?"

"I must be able to see someone in order to transport them."

As Aileen nods in understanding, Beelzebuth spreads his wings. They're black and look as if cloth has been stretched across their bones.

"I'll begin searching."

"Hold on. If the humans see you, Beelzebuth, the uproar will only get worse. I'll go. You can't go, either, Master Claude! Your black hair, red eyes, and pointlessly handsome face will stand out far too much! You're surprisingly famous, demon king!"

"But then we won't have enough people out looking. We don't even know where in the second layer to search."

As she listens to them, Aileen abruptly remembers something.

Come to think of it, wasn't there an event where a demon appeared at the academy...? Yes, it was in Marcus's route! If I recall, Lady Lilia used her powers as the Maid of the Sacred Sword and helped Marcus defeat it—which means we have to hurry!

She has the feeling the demon involved in that event wasn't a young one, so this may only be a coincidence, but being defeated means death. That's far too harsh a penalty for merely getting lost, demon or not.

Claude, who's been standing still with his eyes closed, opens them. Apparently, he's used magic.

"There's no commotion at the academy or among the Holy Knights yet."

"Let's find it while we have the chance, then. I'll help search the academy."

Aileen has raised her hand, and everyone turns their gaze toward her.

"It won't look all that unnatural if I wander about the academy grounds. I'm familiar with the layout, too. Go to the Holy Knights' facility first, if you would, Master Keith."

"Huh? Ah, well... That would be a great help, but..."

"Are you a fool, girl? You will be torn to pieces. Child or not, a fenrir is still a fenrir."

Beelzebuth scoffs at her. She tilts her head, looking perplexed.

"That's true of Master Keith as well, is it not?"

"That child knows Keith and will trust him."

"In that case, lend me an item of Master Claude's clothing. If

it's a magical beast, I'll be able to use the scent to persuade it that
I've come to find it because he wished me to, won't I?"

Since no one objects, she assumes her plan is a good one.
Smiling, Aileen reaches for the tie Claude wears around his neck.
With a soft rustle, the silk comes undone.

"Allow me to borrow this."

She winds the tie around her own wrist.

"Master Claude, will you be able to track my movements?
When I find it, I shall take it to a spot where we won't be seen, so
it would be wonderful if you came to fetch it promptly."

"I can, but... No, wait. In the first place, we don't need your
help."

"Never fear. I won't blackmail you into attending the soiree
if I find it."

"—Then why? You have no reason to help us."

Aileen finds the very question rather appalling.

"What are you saying? It's lost, the poor thing!"

"......"

"Of course, I do intend to put you in my debt and get you to
attend the soiree, but..."

"You do, do you?"

"Yes, I do. However, first of all, I'd like to make your wish
come true."

Claude looks as if she's caught him off guard. She gazes straight
at him.

"In any case, it's only natural for the wife of the demon king
to go to a demon's rescue, correct?"

"—No, wait a minute, why did you just casually slip 'wife' in
there?"

"Come, Master Claude, don't trouble yourself over trivialities. Send me to the academy, if you would."

"'Trivialities' isn't the word I would use."

"Humans are faultfinders by nature. If they find it, they may kill it. Hurry."

When she presses them a little, Beelzebuth goes pale, and Claude's face turns serious.

Aileen has held out her hand. Claude closes his eyes briefly. Then as if he's made up his mind, he takes it.

"…Then I'll leave it to you."

At that husky request, Aileen looks up, startled, but all she sees is the academy's familiar rear garden.

The place is lush, green, and deserted. As she peers around, Aileen smiles.

"Then I'll leave it to you," *he says.*

It really is nice to be relied on. That feeling has tripped her up before, so she doesn't expect anything from it now, but she does want to save the lost young demon.

To be surrounded by humans, cursed at, and killed, when all the fenrir has done is take a less than ideal path. Reminds her of herself.

As the game's main location, the academy is vast. Aileen knows that a haphazard search would only be a waste of energy, and so first, she checks behind the dormitories, where the "demon slaying" event had taken place.

I could just keep an eye on Marcus, but if the demon is discovered before the event occurs, I'll end up a step behind. Besides, if this winds up being unrelated to the event, then following Marcus will be pointless.

Beyond the dormitory's rear gate, there's a stone-flagged road that leads to the Holy Knights' training ground. Marcus, who hopes to join the Holy Knights, secretly sneaks over there to train after school lets out—or so his character profile said. If she remembers correctly, during the event, he encounters the demon on his way there.

If there's no demon near here, she'll have to consider the possibility that the lost young demon has no connection to the event.

"It would be really helpful if it let us find it easily— Oh."

As she approaches the back of the dormitory, she starts to hear a commotion. Nasty laughter and a demon's shrieks.

"Blast! Its horns are hard. Wooden staves won't do a thing."

"Hurry up! We'll kill it while it's stuck in the trap!"

"Hit it first, to weaken it! If we defeat a fenrir, they might even let us into the Holy Knights."

That brief exchange is enough to tell her what's going on. Clenching her fists, Aileen hurries toward the knot of male pupils who have something cornered in the kitchen garden.

At the same time, she hears the voice of a young beast growling and snarling desperately.

"Don't damage its horns or fangs. Fenrir horns and fangs sell for a bundle—"

"What are you doing?"

A shiver runs through the boys' backs. They turn to look, and Aileen quickly checks their faces.

Why, they're all the children of knights. They made fun of Marcus behind his back, calling him a spoiled rich boy—and yet they do this? How pathetic.

Through the gaps between the boys, she can see a white beast, their front leg caught in a bear trap. Their body is small and fluffy, but two sharp horns grow from their forehead, contradicting their otherwise sweet appearance. Their claws are large as well, and they obviously aren't a dog. However, after seeing them struggling frantically to do something about the metal teeth biting into their leg, striking at the creature very much violates the spirit of chivalry.

Aileen gives the boys a sophisticated smile, without hiding her scorn.

"You intend to kill a demon? Are you not aware of the non-aggression pact?"

"L-Lady Aileen... I'd heard you'd left school."

"Don't get s-scared of someone like her..."

Not wanting to waste time dealing with them, Aileen slips between the boys.

If I recall, my brother taught me how to release these...!

She reaches for the trap, and with a growl, the demon leans in and bites her. The fabric of her sleeve tears, and the sound makes the boys shriek.

"I-it got her!"

"Be quiet! This little one is clever."

She's bleeding slightly, but they haven't gouged away any flesh. They must still be holding back. They remember Claude's order.

Aileen draws a breath, then smiles at the growling young demon.

"It's a pleasure to meet you. I am Aileen. I've come to take you home."

Softly, she holds her wrist out to the demon, in front of their nose. The tie sways lightly in the breeze, and the young demon blinks.

"You understand, don't you? Be patient a little longer. If you move around, I won't be able to remove that trap."

The demon gazes steadily at the tie, and there's hesitation in those eyes. However, in the next moment, someone yanks Aileen backward. Her ankle makes an unpleasant noise, and then she lands on her rear.

"What are you doing?!"

"Shut up! It wounded a human, so it's okay if we kill it now!"

The young demon has begun snarling again, all their fur bristling up, and the boys surround them, armed with gardening hoes.

"I told you to stop tha—"

Before she's finished speaking, a shadow swallows her words. Startled, Aileen looks up. In the same moment, the boys give pathetic shrieks and immediately turn on their heels, scattering in all directions.

A demon has appeared, leaping over the wall to land in the garden. The trapped young demon stops crying and gives a sweet, soft whine.

This is the demon from the event... Oh, I see! This youngling is its child!

The demon has disobeyed Claude, crossed the barrier, and come looking for their young. Their eyes are burning with rage.

After seeing this situation, that's only natural. Discovering your child caught in a trap, front leg bloodied, one hind leg bent unnaturally—no parent would doubt who was responsible for those wounds.

Glaring at Aileen, the demon opens their mouth, revealing rows of terrible fangs. Realizing the fenrir is on the verge of howling, Aileen calls out hastily.

"Stop! You mustn't make noise; you'll call people to us!"

Aileen tries to stand but sinks to her knees. Apparently, when that boy had pushed her out of the way earlier, she sprained her ankle. However, she grits her teeth and crawls forward, reaching for the trap.

"I understand that you're angry, but please save it for later. Right now, the child comes first!"

The demon, who hasn't howled after all, glares, looking around. In the meantime, Aileen hastily sets to work on the trap. When she manipulates its components in the order her brother taught her, the clenched jaws compliantly open.

With a soft cry, the young demon tries to go to their parent. Knowing that what she says probably won't get through to them, Aileen speaks to the larger creature.

"Take your child and go somewhere deserted immediately. Master Claude will come to fetch you. No doubt he'll heal those wounds as well. Return to the forest."

"……"

"Go, hurry. I'll handle the rest somehow, so make haste!"

Things are already getting noisy behind her. Once Marcus comes along, armed with his sword, the event will begin. She really doesn't have the strength to fend off Marcus's blade.

The greater demon looks at Aileen steadily but eventually picks up the child by the scruff of their neck and leaps lightly over the wall. Aileen is relieved, but only for the space of a breath.

"—Aileen. What are you doing here? You withdrew from school voluntarily."

She hears Marcus's disdainful voice. Behind him, a group with stern, fierce faces. Lilia is there, too, hanging back rather timidly.

…So it really was the event.

Angered by the fact that their child had wandered in and been hurt, a demon attacked humans and was killed. If the event was something that unfair, then even if it had nothing to do with Aileen's own progress, she's thrilled to have averted it.

Feeling triumphant, Aileen flashes a refined smile.

"I'd forgotten something. I simply came to retrieve it."

"'Forgotten something,' hmm? ...I heard there were reports of a demon here."

"Yes, there was a demon. It was caught in that trap, so I let it go."

"Let it go? As if a duke's daughter would know how to release a beast trap like this one."

He sounds so perfectly convinced of this that she misses her chance to argue.

Well, that's true. Ordinarily, they probably couldn't.

Marcus seems to have misinterpreted her silence. He asks her a question bluntly.

"We received a report that you were tormenting a trapped demon in an attempt to sic it on Lilia."

"—Huh?"

"We're right under Lilia's room here."

When he points this out, Aileen looks up at the dormitory, right beside them.

Are we? she thinks, feeling oddly convinced by the explanation. A laugh works its way up.

"What a ridiculous plan. There are far too many holes, and I'd be more likely to die first."

"Even so, I wouldn't put it past you. As a matter of fact, I heard it had attacked you in self-defense."

She glances past Marcus; the boys who fled a moment ago are

crowded behind him. They probably intend to steal a march on Aileen by pinning the blame for what they did on her. After all, if they told Marcus that, he'd believe it.

Goodness, whatever will we do? I can't visualize a future in which Marcus isn't ruined.

As Aileen smiles coldly, Marcus speaks to her in a harsh tone.

"Are you telling me the daughter of Prime Minister d'Autriche doesn't know that we have a nonaggression pact with the demons?"

"Wait, Marcus. I really can't think that Lady Aileen plotted a thing like that. There's been some kind of misunderstanding. Isn't that right, Lady Aileen? I believe you."

That's a heroine for you. She's got the right answer. Still, how dare she tell the girl whose fiancé she stole that she believes her... There's nothing about her that makes me think I can trust her.

And so Aileen chooses to hold her tongue and not make excuses for herself. It's not clear how Marcus has interpreted this; he merely clicks his tongue in irritation.

"...No damage was done. In deference to Lilia's kindness, I'll let you off the hook this time, but you best hurry and leave the school grounds. Excuse us. Come on, Lilia."

"But, Marcus, isn't Lady Aileen injured?"

"Serves her right. She can just crawl home."

Marcus glances at Aileen's feet. He's probably noticed the injury to her foot as well. He's sharp. With so many regrettable traits, little wonder he's a candidate for the future captain of the Holy Knights.

Still, we've managed to keep this quiet. Having to take the blame for all of it is irritating, but it's not as if I have any reputation left to lose.

Her chest doesn't ache. No doubt it's because she's given up already. As Marcus and the others leave, she gazes absently at their backs... And that's when it happens.

The sky, which has begun to darken into night, warps.

"What in—?!"

Stepping protectively in front of Lilia, Marcus sets a hand on his sword, then freezes.

In the dusky sky, hair as dark as night and a jet-black cloak stream in the wind. Red eyes open slowly.

The figure that's floating in midair can't possibly be human.

"The demon king...?"

"It can't be. I heard he never leaves the forest...," someone murmurs.

Aileen is also staring wide-eyed.

Why is Master Claude here?

There's no reason for him to put in an appearance now.

The demon king descends to earth, toes first, while the humans stand petrified, as if he's bewitched them.

The first one to break free of that spell is Marcus.

"Who are you?! The demon king?!"

"......"

"Answer me... If you don't, I'll assume you're suspicious and arrest you!"

The tip of his sword glints in the evening sun. Before Aileen can protest, though, Claude's sword clips it. Marcus's eyes fly open, but he promptly attacks again.

Aileen's eyes can't follow Marcus's swordplay, but Claude keeps parrying without moving a step or giving his opponent so much as a glance. Even to an amateur, the overwhelming difference in skill is obvious.

"—Dammit! Lilia, stay back."

"A-all right."

"Rrraaaaaaaaaaaaaaaah!!"

Marcus gets a better grip on his sword, then charges, roaring as he surges forward.

However, with a sigh, Claude murmurs, sounding bored.

"Irritating human."

Aileen isn't even able to see what happens next. Then Marcus is laid out on the ground, eyes wide and dazed, with a sword pointed at the base of his throat.

Without having looked at him once, Claude sheathes his sword. When he hears the noise, Marcus screams:

"—Wait, why aren't you finishing me off?!"

"Aileen Lauren d'Autriche."

"Y-yes?"

"You have my gratitude."

Completely ignoring Marcus, Claude places his hand on his chest, bowing his head to Aileen.

An agitated murmur runs through the onlookers. Aileen is just as unsettled. Her mind can't keep up with these developments. Even so, Claude continues.

"When the young fenrir was trapped and frightened, even when you were bitten, you rendered aid without flinching. As the demon king, I have come to thank you in person."

Claude's tone is different from what she usually hears. Aileen understands that he's speaking formally, but not why he's talking to her that way, and as she responds, she's still perplexed.

"Thank me? I didn't do anything worth…"

"In order to avoid precipitating a war with the demons, you even accepted the false accusation that you were the one responsible for hurting the child… For the sad reason that were you the injured party, no one would rise to protect you."

At Claude's words, the people around them mutter, exchanging glances. Marcus frowns, glancing from Aileen to the male students who'd been attempting to kill the young demon earlier.

"The demon you helped is furious at the humans who insulted you, the young fenrir's benefactor."

At that point, Claude turns his gaze on the people behind her. The ones who shudder are, of course, the boys who abused the young demon.

"However, if you wish to pardon them, I will let it pass this time."

As Aileen listens to him, stunned, it finally sinks in.

He came to help me.

He's shown himself in order to clear up the false accusation made against her.

Even though there's no benefit for him in doing that.

"…Yes. Your kind words are more than enough for me."

Putting a hand to her chest, Aileen finally manages a brief response. Claude nods.

"I see. Then I will overlook it—in deference to you."

Stressing his point until the very end, Claude snaps his fingers. Immediately, sparks of light swirl around her.

It's magic. Her ripped clothes revert to their original state, and the mud and grime on the fabric dissolve and vanish. The blood that's caked on her arm and the pain in her leg both disappear as well. It's all happened in mere moments, and both Marcus and Lilia stare, eyes round.

"Does anything hurt?"

"N-no, I'm all right."

"Then I'll see you to your mansion."

Claude snaps his fingers a second time. Instantly, a shining silver carriage appears right beside her.

It's a grand thing, drawn by two black horses with magnificent manes.

"Wh-where did you pull that from?!"

As one would expect, Aileen is startled. Claude looks at her, eyes wide, then gives a faint smile.

Oh.

It's winter, but she can smell flowers. Just now, somewhere, flowers have bloomed. For some reason, she's sure of it.

"It's too soon to be amazed— Your hand, if you will."

Obediently, Aileen puts out her hand. Taking it and drawing her with him, Claude opens the door of the carriage.

"This carriage flies."

"What?"

The horses whinny, unfurling wings from their backs. They're pegasi.

Startled, Aileen involuntarily clings to Claude's waist, and both she and the carriage rise lightly into the air.

Leaving Marcus and the others stunned and openmouthed on the ground, the carriage begins to race toward the dark evening sky.

There is no maiden who does not dream of carriages that course through the air. Aileen gazes out the window at the night sky and the sparkling imperial capital as they fly past.

The stars have begun to twinkle. The gas lamps and the light filtering from the houses below spread out in the shape of a fan.

The colors and lights in the third layer, the commercial district, are more brilliant than the rest.

"How lovely..."

"When you do that, you finally look like an ordinary young woman."

Although Aileen has been pressed to the window, her cheeks flushed, that voice brings her back to her senses. Claude is sitting in the seat directly opposite her, legs crossed. He seems to be observing her, and she clears her throat.

"Don't be rude, please. I *am* an ordinary young woman."

"No ordinary young woman would dose the demon king with aphrodisiacs."

"...But then why did you save me?"

"Because you wouldn't talk back to them, girl!"

Abruptly hearing that voice, Aileen looks around the carriage in confusion. Then she does a startled double take.

Beelzebuth is pressed against the window, on the outside.

"You're ruining the view...!"

"Shut up! Why didn't you defend yourself, girl?! I thought you'd pay them back a million times what you got!"

"Have you gone out of your way to fly here just so you could ask me that?"

"The king told us not to interfere, so we had no choice but to stand back and watch."

"Hear, hear! Girl! Explain!"

The window on the other side is buried in crows. Aileen assumes a serious expression.

"Master Claude. Am I to infer that right now, the air around this carriage...?"

"...Is swarming with demons, yes. What of it?"

"A marvelous journey through the night sky, well and truly spoiled."

"Never mind that, girl, just answer! The king is waiting for your response."

It's quite obviously the demons surrounding the carriage who are waiting for her response.

With a deep sigh, Aileen resettles herself in a well-mannered way, then explains briefly.

"Because it was convenient."

Claude is still gazing at Aileen as quietly as ever. Thanks to that, she's managed to explain herself in a detached way.

"The important thing was to keep the young demon safe and avoid giving the humans a pretext for claiming grievance. If the situation can be resolved smoothly, a little misunderstanding is a small price to pay."

"That...may well be, but..."

"Besides, I couldn't think of a clever way to win them over."

Aileen lets out a contrived-sounding sigh.

"My reputation at the academy is terrible. If I'd told them that those male students had struck first, no one would have believed me, you know? In fact, it would only have worsened my position—"

"No! No!"

"What, do you mean to say I'm lying?"

"Not that. Why didn't you try to get us to corroborate your story?!"

Finding herself the target of unanticipated indignation, Aileen blinks, her long eyelashes rising and falling. Then she murmurs, under her breath.

"If I'd done that, I have the feeling things would have become much more difficult."

"Wh-what do you mean?"

"No matter what you'd say on my behalf, they would only have assumed that I'd deceived demons, and then the situation would have deteriorated that much further—which is to say your concern is uncalled for."

"What?!"

Sour-faced, Beelzebuth leans in closer to the window glass. Aileen casts a ladylike smile at him.

"I mean that I haven't fallen so low that I need you to save me."

"This is why people hate you! Not cute at all!"

"Why, how astute of you. I detest being in debt to others... Although, I love putting them in mine."

"...Beelzebuth. All of you, leave us."

The moment Claude issues his quiet order, Beelzebuth, who's been glaring through the glass, sobers. As if this argument never happened, he gives a polished bow, then winks out of sight.

Once the demons on the opposite side have disappeared as well, it's quiet again in the blink of an eye. At that point, Claude speaks.

"The demons are beginning to warm up to you."

Her eyes go wide.

"To...me?"

"In simple terms of *good* or *bad*, their impressions of you are mostly bad, but you saved the young fenrir. That is why."

"All this because I saved a single child once? They're rather easy, aren't they?"

"Unlike humans, demons don't consider appearances important. You risked yourself to save one of their own. That means everything, and it does not matter what your reasons were. Playing the villain to keep them from caring is rather pointless."

He speaks as if he's seen through everything, and Aileen isn't entirely happy with that, but she does understand.

"They sound as if they'd be easily fooled and pay dearly for it. You must have to keep a very close eye on them, Master Claude."

"You aren't much different."

"Excuse me? No one's fooled me."

Claude doesn't respond. He merely glances at her. His gaze seems to say that he's intentionally avoiding specifics, and her eyebrows come together in a frown.

"If you mean my former fiancé, that's no concern of yours."

"I have learned that you are the type of human who does not cry, make excuses, or ask for help."

With red eyes that seem to be unraveling the mystery in front of him, eyes that hold no sympathy nor anything like it, Claude continues.

"I expect that's why you won't explain the true reason you proposed to me, a man you don't love, who isn't even human. Will you still not tell me?"

"Even if I did, I'm sure you wouldn't believe me."

"I may believe you, or I may not, but that isn't for you to decide."

He has a point. Aileen nods, then smiles.

"I will tell you, then. The truth is, I have memories from my past life."

"Huh?"

"You see, this world is an *otome* game that existed in my previous life. Lady Lilia is the heroine—the protagonist—while I am the aristocratic villainess. I am, as they say, the rival who exists to be vanquished. That broken engagement was, if you'll believe it, the sign of an impending future in which I die. You will kill me, Master Claude, after you've fully assumed the form of a demonic dragon."

"......"

Claude's eyes are cold. Incredibly cold. However, Aileen continues with a smile.

"You've heard of the power of love, though, correct? It occurred to me that, if I hastened to make you mine, I could escape death, and so I proposed to you. How about that? Does any of that make sense?"

"...Yes. You've made yourself quite clear."

Claude's response is unamused, and instantly, the only thing surrounding her is sky. The carriage has vanished.

The night wind strokes her cheeks, and the imperial capital spreads out below her. There's nothing beneath her feet.

Naturally, she falls.

"You still believe I can't understand, and so you mock me. Yes, I understand quite well."

"Ee——"

The fall swallows her scream. She's skydiving, plunging through the gaps in the clouds.

This can't be happening! I'm going to die!

She's so frightened, she can't even shriek. Panicking, Aileen impulsively grabs the arm Claude has extended and wraps her own arms around his neck, clinging to him. Even so, she continues to fall faster and faster.

As she grits her teeth against the wind, which billows up from beneath her, she hears a furtive chuckle right by her ear. Aileen is falling backward, and the night sky fills her vision.

Oh wow—shooting stars.

Her fall abruptly slows.

Claude's shoes descend onto the lawn. Aileen is still hugging his neck, and her feet slowly touch the ground, too, toes first.

She continues her descent, sinking down weakly to sit on the grass—and at the same time, she yells angrily.

"What in heaven's name was that for?! Are you trying to kill me, you fiend?!"

"Well, I am the demon king."

"So you're owning that now, are you?! What on earth did you intend by making me plunge to my death?!"

"I will attend that soiree."

"—What?"

His abrupt consent punctures her anger. Still sitting weakly, she looks up at Claude, who's standing on the lawn.

"Wh-what...happened? That was sudden..."

"Now neither of us owes the other. It's just as you wanted, correct?"

"...Y-yes, but... Why are you smiling?"

"Oh. Am I smiling?"

The man is wearing a sublimely bewitching smile, but apparently, he didn't notice.

"Even I think this emotion is well suited to a demon king."

"Explain— Or no, never mind, I have a rather nasty feeling about this."

"I've begun to want to make you cry."

Her words turn into a faint gasp, as if the air has leaked out of them.

With a light thump, Claude launches himself off the ground, returning to the night sky. Behind him, she can still see falling stars. There are quite a lot of them tonight.

No, that's not it. Claude's emotions are what's making the stars fall. That's why they're shining so brightly.

Wh-what sort of feeling does that?!

Leaving a dazed Aileen in the courtyard of the d'Autriche mansion, the beautiful red-eyed demon king melts into the night sky of a crescent moon.

She's been angling for the route where he falls for her, but perhaps she's ended up on a route where he just bullies her instead.

No, calm down. There was no such route. My memories haven't fully returned yet, but I'm sure that doesn't exist!

Aileen is standing in front of the oven, face serious, arms folded. There's a triangular kerchief tied around her head, and her hands are encased in her favorite mitts.

In the first place, was Master Claude always that sort of character? True, if you only look at the fact that he's supposed to be the demon king, one could easily expect him to be a complete sadist, but I seem to recall he was a touching character with an aura of loneliness and whose kindness worked against him.

"I've begun to want to make you cry."

"Gyaaaaaaaaaaaaaagh!"

"Y-young mistress? Is something the matter?"

"N-no, it's nothing... Watching the oven made me want to scream."

Fluttering her hands to fan her red face, she desperately tries to convince the kitchen servants that nothing is the matter. The servants look mystified, but perhaps because they don't want to get involved, they don't press the issue.

Wiping off the sweat that's broken out on her forehead, she takes several deep breaths.

First, analyze this calmly... To begin with, someone who isn't gorgeous could never get away with a line like that— Curses, Master Claude is *gorgeous!*

That was why that remark sounded so thoroughly indecent, and why she, who has no immunity to these things, has developed such awful palpitations.

It certainly isn't because she's excited—and actually, it would be bad news if she was.

"I refuse to end up on a surprise, depraved S&M route. I'd prefer to avoid one of those 'happy-but-actually-not' endings as well!"

Muttering to herself, she pulls a golden-brown apple pie out of the oven. It's today's gift.

Thinking she should take the opportunity to get ready while the pie is cooling, Aileen leaves the kitchen, letting the servants take care of the rest. When she'd told them that she would be going out earlier, they cheerfully agreed to help.

When one is no longer "the crown prince's fiancée," life is rather carefree.

Before, she paid strict attention to every single place she went. Any sort of clumsy error she happened to make would impinge on Cedric's reputation and honor. Every destination she chose, from the tea parties she attended to the stores she patronized, had to be "suitable for the fiancée of the crown prince."

This was a source of pride for her, but now that she's been released from it, life is easier.

...So much easier that she can't stop being angry about the fact that all she'd done had been for nothing.

"Are you going out, young mistress?"

"Yes, on Father's orders. I'll be going to the third layer, so I won't need a carriage."

That was all she'd needed to say to keep the outstanding servants from asking about her supposed errand.

Having changed clothes, Aileen pulls a cloak around her shoulders and leaves home, keeping her true destination—the demon king's forest—concealed.

The weather is fine again today.

Oh, I've left my parasol at the abandoned castle.

It's currently winter. The fact that those forest demons hadn't been suspicious of her as she walked along with her parasol meant they were tragically naive. No doubt they would be rewarding to train.

"If my way is barred by the barrier again today, perhaps I'll start by demanding the return of my parasol."

"Hey, you over there!"

During the day, she has to be careful to camouflage where she's going. Aileen has descended from the first layer to the third, and she's walking along the paved road, putting her plan together, when a familiar voice hails her.

"Oh, Jasper. Good day to you."

"Yeah, I thought that was you, Miss Aileen. Is your engagement really off?"

Aileen smiles at her reporter acquaintance, who's wearing a shabby jacket. He waves at her casually.

"Yes, it is. Although, I won't give you an interview about it."

"That's not why I was asking. I'm in your debt, miss, and anyway, I'm on the side of justice."

Jasper spins his favorite fountain pen with a grin on his sociable face. Aileen shrugs lightly.

"You're still saying things like that? You're already past thirty, you know."

"Aw, it's fine. In the first place, if I wrote down your gripes about the man, it wouldn't sell as an article for the common folk... Even if it would work as one of those fluff pieces for the aristocrats. Still, though, that was a bum move. After all you did for Prince Cedric— Whoops."

Finding himself on the receiving end of Aileen's cold glance, Jasper covers his mouth with a hand, as if he's realized he's put his foot in it. The man is irritating, but he's quick-witted and skilled at avoiding crises.

Jasper Varie is the president of a small newspaper company in the commercial district, and a man with the spine to delve into any collusion and political corruption transpiring between aristocrats. His paper is written for the common people, and its well-researched articles and unbiased perspective have won it a solid reputation.

Once, when this man was in pursuit of a corrupt aristocratic legislator, Aileen had formed a united front with him. She did so because the legislator had been making use of Cedric's name. In order to prevent the issue from affecting Cedric, Aileen discretely passed information to Jasper, who was covering the incident; in return, he ensured that Cedric wouldn't get dragged into the scandal.

Thanks to that connection, every so often, Jasper makes contact with her and drops nuggets of information. On occasion, Aileen has whispered this information into the ear of her father, the prime minister, and she's also shared valuable information she's learned from her father with Jasper. In short, she's a go-between.

Jasper isn't a character you can interact with in the game, so I think he's probably safe, but...

She wants to keep her interactions with game-related people to a minimum. Just to be on the safe side, she sounds him out.

"...On that note, Jasper, do you know Lady Lilia?"

"Huh? Oh, Master Cedric's lover? Nah, I dunno her personally. I'm not real interested, either."

The answer relieves her. Apparently, she's grown rather paranoid. Mentally, she switches gears.

"I see. That's perfect, then. I have business with you."

"Hang on a sec. Sorry, but I go first. On request, you see. Miss Aileen, you were going to launch construction and transportation businesses while you developed new medicines, weren't you? You said the public infrastructure alone wouldn't be enough."

"Oh, happily, I'm told that's become a public enterprise. I'm not permitted to have anything to do with it now."

"The thing is, the crew you hired came crying to me, saying they'd been fired."

Scratching the back of his neck, Jasper goes on.

"You were efficiently developing useful hygiene products that the common people would be able to afford. In order to better market them, you were going to develop trade routes and transportation, and you were planning to use that as an opportunity to improve the local economy by creating more jobs in shipping and roadbuilding— That was the idea, right? You were trying to give the fifth-layer folk who live hand-to-mouth a bit of regular income. Then the empire's tax revenue would go up, and the people would become more prosperous as a whole."

"That's right."

"Yeah, so I ran help wanted ads to assist you, but... Prince Cedric said they were gonna source all materials from land held by the crown, which meant they wouldn't need transportation or new roads, and he canceled all the construction contracts. None of the roads or anything had been built yet, so the money just evaporated."

"Were the cancellation penalties paid properly?"

Aileen has stepped in closer. Jasper shakes his head.

"Nope. Apparently, Master Cedric told 'em he wouldn't even cover the starting costs, since the business he thought up wouldn't use that stuff... I hear Master Rudolph managed to get a budget for the work they'd completed, at least, but that won't pay for a while, either."

"Father did..."

Now she understands why her father had decided to disregard Cedric, and the reasons for the anger behind his reckless demand.

...Although, it's extremely likely that the reason he didn't tell her he was cleaning up after her was not out of consideration, but because he was looking forward to her finding out and feeling bad about it later.

"It's not like anybody's gonna starve right this minute, but it was a big, long-term job, see. Nobody picked up other work or had anything else lined up, and they're hurting. Got any decent leads? They'd settle for the charity you nobles specialize in."

"Don't be ridiculous; charity wouldn't help the economy, and it would eventually compromise the nation's future."

She cuts him off flatly, and for some reason, Jasper smiles.

"I like that side of you, y'know."

"We'll have to find them work where they'll receive fair pay, or— Oh."

The idea that's abruptly occurred to her makes her curve her lips into a smile. Jasper backs away.

"Wh-what's that face for?"

"Listen, is it possible that Master Cedric's let all the people I selected go?"

"Uh, yeah. He said he couldn't trust people chosen by Aileen Lauren d'Autriche, especially not fifth-layer folk... I dunno if it's okay for a crown prince to be saying stuff like that; do you?"

"...From what I hear, he's stopped trying to keep up appearances."

He must have been supportive only on the surface, simply because he thought it didn't matter, while inwardly snidely laughing at her and her subordinates. In other words, this is what he really thinks of them.

"Well, I think it's probably just jealousy."

"What do you mean?"

"You know. For some reason, lots of the supervisors you appointed were young, good-looking men. I think maybe he didn't want to let them near Lady Lilia. The guy's head over heels for her."

He'd let that kind of talent go for a reason like that? Aileen widens her eyes in utter amazement.

However, just this once, she's grateful for his foolishness; it means the people she wants are still available.

"Still, that's saved me the trouble of asking you, then. The personnel were the one thing I didn't have a plan for."

"Hmm? You've got something else up your sleeve?"

"Father's told me to recoup our losses."

Jasper's eyes go round. Then he whistles.

"That's Prime Minister d'Autriche all over. No mercy, even for his daughter. Or no, maybe that's why?"

"Tell everyone who was let go that if they'd like, you'll set them up with another job. I have to set about restoring a castle. I'd also like to have a carriage made. It's going to be a rush job, so the pay will be generous."

"You mean it? They're gonna be thrilled; that's a huge help. Besides, the supervisors are, well, you know."

"The work will be rough, though. Tell them that only those willing to take on any job at all should come forward."

"Eh, I wouldn't worry. They've got solid skills; you hand-picked them yourself. Work opportunities just tend to pass them by due to prejudice, since they're from the fifth layer, and because they're a motley bunch of characters who don't just meekly obey any order they're given."

"That's fine, then. Also, about the medicine... I have an idea there as well. Can I arrange the meeting place and time through you, as we generally do? Assemble the usual members first."

"Sure, I'm on it."

"In addition, I have one more request for you... Sir Ally of Justice."

When she addresses him, Jasper instantly looks pleased.

"What's this? A scoop?"

"Are you familiar with a high-ranking official named Keith? He's the demon king's attendant, and I believe he's rather famous."

"Yeah, well, I mean... Uh, Miss Aileen? Why'd you bring up the demon king all of a sudden?"

"His salary isn't being paid. I'm not certain, but I believe someone may be misappropriating the entire budget that's intended for the demon king."

Jasper widen his eyes, and then he lowers his voice.

"Is that for real? Maybe he's the demon king, but the man's still a prince. They must have a pretty good stipend set aside for him, even if it's only so he won't become miserable and sic the demons on 'em."

"That was what I'd assumed as well, but..."

The decrepit abandoned castle rises behind her eyelids. She really can't believe its current state is the result of a generous stipend.

"For now, do look into it. We may stumble upon something big. After all, it is the demon king's budget."

Ordinarily, no one would even consider embezzling a thing like that. In other words, it has to be someone who's known from the start that Claude wouldn't file a complaint against them. In any event, they're bound to be far from ordinary.

Looking grave, Jasper nods.

"All right, I'll look into it. We're using the same contact method as always?"

"Yes, I'll make a submission to the newspaper. Respond to my summons with an advertisement, if you would."

"Roger that. Still, the demon king, huh...? Not bad: *The forbidden prince who was stripped of his right to the throne!*"

"If you stand for justice, the demon king is your enemy. Isn't this rather complicated for you?"

When she asks him a leading question, trying to gauge his true feelings, Jasper waves a hand from side to side adamantly.

"No, not at all. Ever since he was a kid, he's had all sorts of attempts made on his life, and he still stays holed up in that abandoned castle, without sending his pack of demons after anybody. He's a real good prince. There's hardly any antidemon measures in place for the fourth and fifth layers, and folk there have more respect for the demon king than the knights. They say it's thanks to him that the demons don't cause trouble anymore."

"...My, is that true?"

"Yeah, the demon king's real popular with the lower classes. This demon will show up, saying, 'Witness the power of demons, feeble humans' and 'Grovel before the king,' but then his crew clears roads that'd been blocked by heavy rainstorms or cleans up demolished buildings. I hear they respond faster than the knights to jobs like that."

That sounds like Beelzebuth for sure. She presses her fingers to her temples, wondering if there aren't slightly better words for him to use.

Still, Master Claude... What a softhearted— Or rather, really, this is...

His ability. Isn't that what it is? He's an able statesman.

Aileen breaks out in goose bumps.

It's a remnant from her dream of becoming the special subject known as *empress.* Aileen shakes her head, dispelling the idle thought that inevitably occurs to her. She doesn't have that kind of luxury right now.

"In that case, if the demon king is close to the lower classes, a story about nobles misappropriating his assets to line their own pockets should go over quite well."

"Yep. The thing is, though, the demon king won't take center stage. I hear he's a stunner, the sort you never forget once you've seen him. If we got photos, I bet he'd be a hit with the ladies, but..."

"I'll put that on the table as a pending issue of the greatest importance... All right—please take care of what we've discussed."

"Will do. By the way, Miss Aileen, what are you going to do?"

"I have somewhere to go."

"And I'm also curious about where that might be, but what I'm asking about is the future. Are you giving up on Prince Cedric? I was looking forward to you becoming empress."

There's no sarcasm in the way he says it, so it doesn't irritate her. In fact, this man once pointed out people she should be wary of when she became the empress and gave her all sorts of other advice. At this point, the day when that information would prove useful will never come—but...

If I survive, that sort of day might come again.

To that end, what she needs to do right now is obvious.

"I have other plans. I've found a man who's better than Master Cedric."

"—Wha...? Nah, wait, it's only been three days since he broke your engagement, right?!"

"Why, love has nothing to do with time."

Suppressing a smile, Aileen walks on elegantly.

"Women are scary," Jasper says, but she pretends she hasn't heard him.

"And so let us repair this castle. We'll use my allowance."

Having reached the abandoned castle without being hindered by the barrier, Aileen cheerfully opens negotiations.

Clear sunlight pours into the parlor, the castle's one functional room, and it's slightly brighter than usual. On her way here, she also noticed there were many small flowers blooming out of season along the track through the forest, so perhaps Claude is in a good mood... Although, from what she can see, his face is as expressionless as ever.

The very first one to respond is Beelzebuth, who's as underdressed as ever.

"You're telling us to allow mere humans into the castle?! Show some respect, girl!"

"It's much less respectful to allow your king to live in a dilapidated castle, you know."

" 'Dilapidated'? You must mean *awesome*! To think you can't see how great this place is... That's the trouble with humans."

Oh, he's one of those desperately edgy types. Instantly giving up on persuading Beelzebuth, who strangely seems as if he's bragging, Aileen turns to Keith, who's capable of having a proper conversation.

"What do you think, Master Keith? It's a good idea, is it not?"

"True, it is awfully drafty in here, and it would be nice to renovate the castle, but... I really don't know about paying from your allowance, Miss Aileen. What's the interest rate?"

"I won't charge any. Master Claude can be the collateral."

"Wow, that is truly inhumane. Count me in!"

"Who's collateral now?"

Claude is seated in an armchair, resting his chin in his hand. He looks rather appalled. From the fact that no wind is blowing and the flowers aren't wilting, he seems to have gotten used to Aileen.

Beelzebuth cocks his head, perplexed.

"What's a collateral...?"

"For a wife, it's her husband."

"No, that's really and truly too much, Miss Aileen..."

"Master Claude, please do allow for repairs to the castle. Think of it as helping those in need. It isn't a bad deal for you, either, you know."

When finally she turns the conversation his way, Claude recrosses his legs. His face is still expressionless.

"...It isn't possible to have humans repair the demon king's castle. I don't intend to leave myself in your debt, and in any case, the demons don't need this—but even if I point these things out, no doubt you have arguments prepared already."

Aileen absolutely does have several replies ready, and having him call attention to them in advance leaves her at a loss.

"I do have some actually, but..."

"In that case, let me put it this way. What reason do you, a duke's daughter, have to personally take on a project like this?"

"Because—it will help those in need."

Claude gives her a look from under his half lowered eyelids. Feeling uncomfortable, Aileen adds to her explanation.

"It's also a chance to retaliate against Master Cedric."

"I believe you blustered about not wanting to waste a single second more of your life on Cedric."

The man has an excellent memory. Aileen decides to change her line of attack.

"As I intend to keep you as a pet, Master Claude, it is my role to provide you with a life of comfort."

"If you won't answer honestly, then forget about it. This is a waste of time. I use the barrier to observe humans who come and go, but I make sure they enter and exit quietly. I don't want to attract the attention of those nagging aristocrats."

"O-of course, I'll be careful... Wait, then it's all right? If I begin the repairs, I mean."

"Yes. Your methods may be one thing, but I trust the results of what you're trying to achieve."

He simply states his opinion as it is, and Aileen, who was ready and eager to talk him around, falls silent, the wind taken out of her sails.

"Keith. Your wages and my stipend are both overdue, aren't they? Pull some strings and gather some capital. We'll put it toward the costs."

"Oh-ho. My first job in quite a while. I'll go give it my best."

Claude issues instructions as if he's used to taking charge, and it flusters Aileen.

"Um, excuse me! I'm acquainted with a journalist named Jasper, and I've asked him to look into that..."

"You've taken steps already? I see. So you never intended to use me as collateral."

Aileen groans a little; he's seen through her as though it's the easiest thing in the world.

He's correct: First, Aileen will put up the funds. Then she'll have Jasper acquire evidence and either threaten or expose the embezzler. Then the money will be sent to Claude and the others. Once that's done, Aileen will be able to reclaim the money she originally fronted.

Her calculations were rough—she merely estimated the total amount that had been withheld, using the figures she remembered—but even after paying for the renovations, Claude and his people should have a decent amount left over. However, she had the feeling that Claude wouldn't accept the money she'd helped him collect unless it was in the form of a loan.

"You really are devious."

Summing up Aileen's intentions in a word, Claude glances at Keith, who's standing off to the side behind him.

"Keith. Can we trust this Jasper fellow?"

"He's the president of the Varie Newspaper, isn't he? He writes good, spirited articles. I think Miss Aileen's choice is quite sound."

"...You do know an awful lot, don't you?"

"I am the demon king's left-hand man, after all. Well then, for the first time in ages, I believe I'll leave for work."

Keith chuckles, and Aileen frowns. She has the feeling that Keith is a force to be reckoned with. He was depicted as a capable retainer who shouldn't be underestimated in the game as well, but in person, he's deeply unsettling.

Naturally, a mediocre, less-than-capable human could never survive in human society as the demon king's adviser.

She understands this rationally speaking, and yet somehow, it's still galling.

"—You're uncomfortable with owing others, aren't you?"

She's barely noticed that a shadow's fallen over her before she registers Claude's face right in front of her own. Aileen gasps, startled, then protests in an unsteady voice.

"A-are you trying to harass me, Master Claude?!"

"Mm, yes. I'm hoping to see you cry."

Gritting her teeth against that devilish whisper, she puts some distance between them. Restraining her heart, which is pounding madly, she speaks as calmly as she can.

"Then I'll ask you for one thing more, Master Claude. Would you loan me some of the land in your possession, including part of the forest? I will pay rent, of course. I'd like to set up a small farm."

"You mean you want to allow humans in here long-term?"

"...Yes. If my project succeeds, that is what would happen."

"You may try it. However, if it causes trouble with the demons, as with the castle renovation, I'll have them leave part-way through."

Taken the other way around, if it looks as though they'll be able to get along with the demons, there will be room for discussion. She must not disregard the things that Master Claude, as the demon king, must dedicate the most attention toward.

"All right. So you'll wait and see how it goes during the castle repairs… That's what you're saying, isn't it?"

"And also how honestly you can ask."

"…Why do you say 'honestly'? I'll pay a fair price."

"I'm not much interested in prices. However, you aren't good at asking honestly, are you?"

Aileen is irritated. She rises to her feet, glaring at Claude, who's saying things that could be either sweet or biting as if they don't bother him at all.

"I'll get right to work, then. Master Beelzebuth!"

"Wh-what?"

"Show me around the castle, if you would. I'll think about how best to repair it."

"Aileen."

"What?!"

She whirls around. The tip of Claude's index finger is glowing faintly. However, his shining fingertip only points in Aileen's direction and traces a line from side to side. Then the light vanishes.

Dubiously, she glances left and right, moving only her eyes. Something feels strange. The source of that unsettling feeling is coming from the shadow beneath her feet. There's a hole in it.

"Wha…? Wh-what?!"

The shadow swells, the hole splits open, and sharp claws, thick forelegs, and a torso that's clearly far bigger than the shadow crawl out. She manages to limit her reaction to backing up rapidly only because she recognizes the creature.

"You're...that young fenrir..."

"I've made your shadow into a gateway for the demons. Now they will be able to emerge from behind you at any time, as they please."

Claude says something outrageous as if it means nothing.

"Wait just a moment. Exactly what do you think you're doing to my shadow?"

"This way, no matter how you move around, the demons won't mind it."

In other words, they'll be keeping an eye on her. When she hears that, there's nothing more she can say. Aileen gazes at her shadow.

Once the fenrir's bushy tail emerges, the shadow reverts to Aileen's shape, and the split vanishes. The young fenrir does an agile flip in midair before making a smooth landing.

There's no sign of a wound, and their fur, which was rather grubby, is now glossy. Their small eyes shine with bright curiosity, and they're obviously healthy and happy. Inwardly, she's relieved, but she frowns.

"Little one, you mustn't stand on that. Get down, please."

The young fenrir blinks at her; they're standing on a table. Figuring that she needs to explain, Aileen decides to crouch down, putting herself on eye level with the fenrir, and points at the floor again.

"That's bad manners. Please get down."

The gesture seems to have gotten through; the young fenrir hops down from the table. Then they puff out their chest proudly, as if saying, *How's that?!* It makes her smile.

"You're a clever little one. Quite promising."

"Yip."

"If you're feeling indebted to me for what happened earlier, there's no need. The humans involved were clearly scum. They were pathetic... And you were truly a good child."

The young fenrir cocks their head, then presses it against Aileen's chest, as if telling her to pet them. Smiling wryly, Aileen obliges.

Seeming satisfied, the fenrir dashes off. They stop in front of the parlor door, then turn to look at Aileen. As she blinks, puzzled, Beelzebuth comes to stand beside them.

That reminds Aileen of what she's been planning to do.

"Are you going to show me around the castle as well?"

"That child wants to thank you for the rescue and also wants to accompany you."

At Claude's words, she looks from the young fenrir to Beelzebuth and back again. Beelzebuth snorts.

"King's orders. Let's go, girl. How long do you plan to keep us waiting?"

"Two lacke...I mean, knights. How splendid."

"Yip!"

"Kn-knights?"

The young fenrir pricks up their big ears, and Beelzebuth's gaze wanders as if he's flustered.

From a short distance away, Keith speaks up.

"Oh, Beeel, before Miss Aileen called you that, she started to call you a lack—"

"Come, Master Beelzebuth. At times like this, you should open the door for me. It's a rule of chivalry."

"When the king goes through a door, it opens on its own. Humans are a real pain."

"I am a delicate damsel. If you are a knight, you should go out first and make sure there is no danger."

"Is that how it goes...?"

"Yes, of course. In the first place, the young fenrir can't open doors. As the demon king's right-hand man, you must show your junior how it's done!"

"I see!"

"Master Claude... Are you sure this is all right?"

"As long as they're enjoying themselves, I don't mind."

Having gained Claude's permission, Aileen walks through the door Beelzebuth has opened.

"Can you close it, little one?"

Eyes shining, the young fenrir gives the door a solid kick with their front legs. The door slams shut loudly. Apparently, they can't control their strength yet.

"...Next time, let's teach you how to close it quietly, shall we?"

"Yip!"

"Let's move, girl. Don't get full of yourself just because the king has taken a liking to you."

"Master Claude has taken a liking to me? He has demons watching me from my shadow..."

"The demons have taken an interest in you, so he's being considerate and telling the ones who want to meet you to go ahead and do so. If they're interested in you, it means the king is as well."

A few steps down the corridor, Beelzebuth turns around.

"He remembered your name, didn't he?"

Come to think of it, she does seem to remember him calling her name for the first time a moment ago.

At the time, she didn't even notice it, but now that it's been pointed out so plainly, her cheeks grow hot. It's just the way it used to be when she was a child, and her father or older brothers or Cedric—anyone she respected—noticed her.

When he sees this, Beelzebuth looks dubious.

"Strange woman. The things you do are shameless, and yet you blush over this?"

"Wha—?!"

"Well, that doesn't matter. Now bow your head! This is the room of our king!"

He must be dying to brag about it. Looking gleeful, Beelzebuth pushes open a pair of double doors.

...Where's the sense in showing me the location of the highest-ranking individual's room without a single thought for security?

I really will have to train him as we go, Aileen thinks with a sigh, calming down all at once.

"...Yeah, I figured you were somebody special, miss."

As he pushes up his beret with his fountain pen, Jasper shouts:

"But who orders repairs on the demon king's castle?! From humans, even!! Are you sure this is fine?!"

"It won't break any laws. You can be sure of that; I stayed up all night researching it."

"Before all the legal stuff, though...! Argh, we're not gonna get eaten, are we?! Seriously, is this okay?"

"I imagine those who are frightened won't come. There's no changing that. Some will, though. Just as you have."

When Aileen points this out, Jasper looks as if she's caught him by surprise.

She and Jasper are still alone in the abandoned castle's ominous courtyard. That's only to be expected; there's half an hour left before the time their group agreed to assemble.

"Well... I'm a bachelor with no family to worry about, and I guess you could say my journalist's nature makes me leap without looking whenever I get wind of a scoop. The other guys, though..."

"Those in the fifth layer are grateful to the demon king— It was you who taught me that."

"Huh? So this is my fault?!"

"I didn't say that... However, Master Claude is..."

He's still trying to protect the humans—his people. Claude's actions may stem from his dream.

There's wishful thinking in those words, and Aileen voluntarily seals them.

"If they don't come, I'll think of another way. After all, my noble rank is riding on this. I'm desperate."

"Your rank, huh...? Sure, I get why you'd be reckless, Miss Aileen. Prime Minister d'Autriche is asking for the moon. I mean, since it's you, you'll probably manage, but still."

"I couldn't. I'm the sort of naive young lady who'd gamble on your information."

Aileen laughs, and Jasper clicks his tongue in exasperation.

"In that case, since I'm the guy who sent you that information, I have to tell you they're bound to come."

"Heh-heh, yes, you see? I may not look it, but I do trust you."

"—Master Cedric's a real idiot, isn't he? Letting a good woman like you get away."

"My, flattery? That's not like you."

"If you do get demoted to commoner, lemme know right away. I'll hunt up a job and a place for you to live."

Aileen is startled. Avoiding her eyes, Jasper adjusts his beret, pulling it down low. A wind blows between them, rustling. It's a strong wind that doesn't suit the clear sky.

"…Well, you'd probably be too much for me to handle anyway."

"Hey, girl! Give me a status report!"

Beelzebuth appears from high in the air, wings spread. Scared, Jasper backs up.

"A—a demon…!"

"There's no need to worry; he's easily managed… Master Beelzebuth, it isn't yet time for everyone to assemble."

"Then which do you think is a more fitting entrance for the king's right-hand man: flying down from on high with a retinue of demons, or incinerating the whole area in a show of power, then appearing by myself?"

"Flying down from on high would be prefe—I mean, more impressive. After all, humans can't fly."

"I see. I will propose it to the king. Also, you. Human."

"Yessir?! Do you mean me, sir?!"

Jasper's voice cracks. Beelzebuth nods magnanimously.

"Yes. Are you our foe?"

"P-perish the thought, sir! I'm just a humble journalist, Miss Aileen's gofer."

"Then refrain from displeasing the king any further. He knows all that happens inside the barrier—and the king can easily send a puny human flying with a simple blast of wind."

Leaving Jasper, who is darting his eyes about in confusion, Beelzebuth flies off toward the other side of the castle.

Wind? Displeased…with Jasper?

Did he mean the wind that had blown suddenly a moment ago? She can't think of an obvious reason why…

"Jasper, did you do something to Master Claude?"

"No way! I've never even seen the demon king!"

"That's true… I wonder what that was about, then. We can't have the weather worsening on us…"

"Oh, is this the thing about how when the demon king gets upset, the result is wind or rain or lightning? …Uh."

Jasper has been thinking hard, too, but abruptly, he looks Aileen right in the face.

"…What about you, Miss Aileen? You've met the demon king, right?"

"Of course I have."

"Huh… Then wait, could that have been—? Is that what that was? Oh…"

Even as Jasper racks his brain, he takes a deliberate step away from Aileen for some reason.

"…What? If you've figured something out, tell me."

"Nah, it's against my principles as an ally of justice to release unconfirmed hunches. There's still a bit of a breeze blowing, too… Is this the demon king's intimidation tactics?!"

"Master Claude wouldn't do a thing like that for no reason."

The moment she says those words, the wind dies. However, Aileen doesn't notice; she's seen the figures she's been waiting for.

More and more shapes appear, walking down the bright track through the forest. Jasper whistles.

"They came, huh? That's you all over, miss: lots of enemies, but a few elite allies."

"Denis, Luc, Quartz—and Isaac, even! I never dreamed you'd come. You're technically an aristocrat, you know."

"Hey, I didn't want to."

Although most of the group is wearing rather grubby clothes, the even-featured youth who steps forward is clearly dressed like a young nobleman. He scratches his head in an irritated way.

"But we're talking about *the* demon king, right? And that makes me wonder what the heck you're doing, see? We're all here because we were worried."

"My, thank you. There's no need to worry about me, though."

"I figured you'd say that, but… Man, your ideas are as crazy as ever. Listen up: Right now, all you need to do is behave, back off, and spend your time weeping. Appearances matter, got it? Then while you're attracting sympathy, you cook up a plan behind the scenes to yank the rug out from under those two."

Isaac rudely points his finger right at her nose and doesn't mince words. She simply snorts at him.

"That's your particular area of expertise, isn't it? I'll leave the mind games to you."

"Oh, what, you're making me do it?! If it's gonna be on me, then try listening to me for a change, wouldja?!"

Isaac Lombard is a fellow pupil at Aileen's academy. He's the third son of Count Lombard, an upstart aristocrat who'd made a success of himself in commerce and purchased a title with money. That's all; there's nothing else particularly notable about Isaac as a character.

He doesn't have any appearances in the game, either. He's only mentioned as one of Marcus's relatives.

Since the title was purchased, he and Marcus aren't related by blood, and because their personalities are polar opposites, they mutually ignore each other. While Marcus is popular and generally stands out, Isaac probably only registers as the sort of unremarkable student you'd find just about anywhere.

Even Aileen wouldn't have paid much attention to him if she

hadn't happened to draw his name in a lottery for a paired assignment. Lilia had drawn Cedric's name in that same lottery; fate in this world is a funny thing.

"I told you up and down that Prince Cedric wasn't the kind of guy you thought he was, remember?"

"Come to think of it, where were you during that soiree?"

"Watching it. From a distance."

"...You watched that. I see."

"Like I could actually have saved you? Come on—the crown prince. Marcus Cowell. Literally the only person who could tick off those two and still have a life is you. If I'd gone out there, I would have died for nothing. It would've been a waste of my sense of justice."

"I know. That instinct is one of the things I trust about you— You let Prince Cedric fire you, didn't you?"

Isaac's family had already put him in charge of their trade, and when Aileen launched her own business, she snagged him. When it comes to the flow of money, Isaac is more familiar with the actual day-to-day management than she is. Not only that, but even if he is nouveau riche, he's also an aristocrat. She can't imagine why Cedric wanted to drive him off.

"...I must've had the sort of face Lady Lilia likes, that's all."

Isaac's answer is brusque, and she laughs at him. Isaac, who has sharp features and eyes that default to glaring, definitely belongs in the *handsome* category. It's only that he seems like a delinquent, and it makes him hard to approach, so no one makes a fuss about him.

A boy with a small frame and winsome features shrugs in a rather mature way.

"Isaac blew up at the prince and left voluntarily."

"Hey, Denis, don't say stuff nobody needs to hear. He's the one who told me I was fired."

"You have my thanks as well, Denis. If you're here, I can relax and leave the on-site supervision to you. How is your master?"

"Doing well, thank you! Thanks to your suggestion to Prime Minister d'Autriche, there's a clinic in the fifth layer now, too."

This boy, whose merits are his slight build and his agility, is a skilled craftsman from the fifth layer. An orphan, he'd been taken in by the artisan he simply calls master and once built a whole house as a way to entertain himself. He's good with his hands, and although he hasn't received much in the way of education, he's a genius architect who can draw up blueprints while also boasting a sophisticated aesthetic sense. She met him when she'd gone along on one of her father's inspections of the fifth layer.

Then Aileen turns to the man who's employed at the clinic that Denis's master frequents.

"And you, Luc. I'm sorry this happened. Just when we'd begun to turn a profit, and it finally looked as if we'd be able to develop the medicines you'd been hoping for..."

"No, no. In terms of my interests as a doctor, I'm more excited about the demon king's forest. I suspect we'll make some new discoveries there. Isn't that right, Quartz?"

Luc is holding his remarkably curly hair back as the wind tugs at it. As he speaks, he turns to his childhood friend.

That young man, who wears an eye patch and a vinegary expression, has his back to them, his arms folded.

"......"

"At least say hello, Quartz."

"It's all right. Thank you for coming, Quartz. I'm sorry I can't take you to the farms of the d'Autriche duchy. I hope the plants of the demon king's forest will be enough to pique your interest."

"......"

"...Is he angry, perhaps?"

The youth Aileen is addressing has clean-cut features and wears his long hair pulled back. She's aware that he almost never speaks, but lately, he began to greet her at least, so this much silence makes her nervous. Luc laughs.

"It's fine, Lady Aileen. What he's angry about is the fact that Prince Cedric took away the plants he'd diligently bred for you."

The taciturn Quartz is a botanist who truly cherishes the plants he grows. He loves his plants so much that she had difficulty persuading him to use them for her business. That was precisely why she insisted on recruiting him and his plants.

"I really am sorry about that. The formulas you and Luc devised were taken as well, weren't they...?"

"That's all right. It isn't your fault, Lady Aileen. Right, Quartz?"

"...Yeah."

When Quartz finally answers, she feels relieved.

"In that case, will the two of you work under me, even in the demon king's forest?"

"Yes, of course."

After Luc responds, Quartz also gives a small nod. These two had both been born and raised in the fifth layer, but their wits won them places as scholarship students at a school in the fourth layer. They're both brilliant, and having them on her team is incredibly reassuring.

"Thank you, truly. I'll be counting on you."

"We'll do our best. And don't worry; if it comes down to it, I'll develop a poison that leaves no traces. Won't I, Master Isaac?"

"Hey, don't arbitrarily set me up as your ringleader, you scheming doctor! I'm not plotting the crown prince's assassination, get me? That stuff's not in!"

"...If there are good materials in the demon king's forest, sure."

"Knock. It. Off! Denis, stop those plant freaks!"

"Hmm. How about a bridge that breaks when it's subjected to more than a certain load instead...?"

"So you want an assassination, too, huh?!"

"Uh... That aside, we should probably start talking business. It's getting real windy out here. And cold!"

Jasper has been quiet until now, but at his suggestion, Aileen glances up at the sky. The wind really has grown stronger, and it's even brought clouds in with it.

"It was sunny just a moment ago... What should we do? You see the state the castle's in. There's nowhere to put a group this size."

"Aaaaand this is where I finally come in!"

A hand shoots up from the very back of the group. Startled, Aileen turns around.

"Master Keith! What are you doing there?"

"I infiltrated and watched to see how things were going for a while. I tell you, this is better than I'd imagined. You've given me quite the shock."

"...Who's that?"

"The demon king's attendant."

At Isaac's answer, everyone turns around. Keith chuckles.

"There's nothing to fear. I'm an ordinary human...like

yourself, Isaac Lombard, third son of the Lombard Company, formerly the Schmidt Trading Company. You're a troublemaker who's rumored to outmatch your older brothers in terms of wits. So you're the brains of Miss Aileen's operation, are you? It's a pleasure to meet you."

"...Thanks. I'm just an accountant, though."

"You're famous as well, Master Denis. A genius who does everything from blueprints to design work. I hear many nobles have courted you to work exclusively for them."

"Heh-heh! I'm just doing whatever I want, that's all."

"Masters Luc and Quartz are outstanding minds, the pride of the fifth layer. The clinic they run together has a tremendously good reputation for its fair prices and excellent outcomes. You're also popular in your own rights."

"You flatter me. Thank you very much."

"...It's just how things turned out."

"But perhaps you're the most impressive one, Miss Aileen. To be able to attract so much talent and assemble this many humans in front of the demon king's castle. No one's ever managed to do that before."

Casually displaying his eloquence, Keith comes right up to Aileen. From beneath his beret, Jasper speaks to him in a low voice.

"I'd heard you stayed cooped up in the forest with the demon king, but... You know quite a bit. You may have more intel than I do."

"Well, I am the demon king's attendant. It's only natural that I'd collect information."

After flashing him a rather insolent smile, Keith looks up at the swaying trees.

"Oh, this won't do. We've chatted for too long and irritated Master Claude. It looks like it may rain."

With that, he moves to stand in front of the iron door of the dilapidated castle.

"Master Claude, I humbly request that you find some way to keep your guests from getting rained on. Come now, everyone. I'll show you in."

Keith bows deferentially to Aileen and the others. At the same time, the iron door opens of its own accord.

A torn banner of the nation flaps in the cloudy sky above the castle, whipped up by the strong wind. It's a scene straight from a horror story.

Wearing the same expression she wore when she first came to this castle, Aileen swallows hard. Even so, she's the first one to step forward. She's the representative here.

With a sigh, Isaac follows her, and Denis follows him, seeming a little skittish. Grimacing, Jasper starts forward as if he's chasing them. Luc and Quartz exchange glances, then go after him. In the rear, the people they've brought trail in, some seeming frightened, others putting on a bold front.

No one's getting cold feet at this point. Once he's confirmed that, Keith turns around.

"Miss Aileen, you really do show promise."

Faintly, ever so faintly, he curves his lips, tracing a smile.

"I do believe I've taken a liking to you."

The dark corridor runs on, illuminated only by the glow of candles. Denis is the first one to voice his doubts.

"That's weird. The place wasn't built like this from the outside..."

"It's probably the demon king's magic. Thinking about it isn't gonna tell you which version's right."

Isaac is probably correct.

Finally, they come upon another set of double doors. These also open on their own.

The moment they step inside, it's so bright that they shut their eyes.

The polished marble floor shines under silver chandeliers, reflecting the light. The ceiling, which is so high that they can't see it unless they crane their necks, is adorned with a glass rose window. They can hear the rain lashing against it. White space stretches away extravagantly to the left and right, and a velvet carpet runs across the room right up to the throne.

It's a king's chamber. The space is equal to that in the Ellmeyer's Empire's royal castle, and the unique atmosphere makes Aileen stand straighter.

Only Claude is there, seated on the throne. His legs are crossed; he's resting his chin on one hand, and his long eyelashes are lowered.

"Master Claude. I've brought your guests."

At the sound of Keith's voice, Claude open his eyes. With that deep-red gaze, like rubies, he peers down at everything.

"So that's...the demon king," Isaac murmurs under his breath.

Keith, who's stolen away from the back of the group, goes to stand at the left of Claude's throne. Simultaneously, Beelzebuth slips through the glass ceiling, unfurls his wings, and descends to a position on the throne's right.

The arrangement makes it clear that this is the demon king and his two most trusted advisers.

Oh good. Master Beelzebuth made a fairly normal entrance.

If it's because Claude restrained him, she's grateful. Beelzebuth has the same sort of supernatural beauty as Claude, and now she knows that, as long as he's just standing there silently, he's terribly imposing.

"There is only one thing I want from you, gentlemen. Do not harm the demons or upset their day-to-day lives."

Claude, who's still resting his chin in his hand, sounds skeptical.

"In addition, as we are inside the barrier, I will be clearly aware of nearly everything you do. Unless I consciously watch and listen, I won't know specifics; conversely, if I decide to, I can do so to an unlimited degree— Keep that in mind. Keith."

"Yes, yes. You'll be paid the amounts that Lady Aileen has indicated to you. It won't be an illusion or anything like that, so rest assured."

"Um… May I ask a question…? Er, I was told we'd be repairing the castle. What about it needs repairing?"

Denis peeks out from behind Isaac. Claude snaps his fingers. Immediately, the alabaster throne vanishes, and the decrepit one Aileen is used to seeing appears.

"Huh? Wha—?"

"Agh, agh, agh, agh, rain! It's raining!"

"—And now you see. No one wants to get rained on, correct? There are many, many things to repair."

With another snap of his fingers, Claude returns the room to normal. In other words, he's just explained that this awesome space was created by magic.

The group has been drenched by the downpour, if only for a

moment, and they all look miserable. Luc shakes the raindrops off his hands.

"Hmm... Should we thank you for your consideration...?"

"...When the weather's rough, plants don't grow well..."

"You will just have to do what you can. I'll also endeavor to keep it as calm as possible."

As he speaks, Claude sweeps his hand to one side. Instantly, everyone is dry again. Looking down at his coat, which is no longer wet or even damp, Isaac mutters:

"Whoa... So that's magic, huh? That's way too handy."

"That is all I have to say. Are there any other questions?"

"Oh, yes! What sort of castle should I build?"

When the talk turns to architecture, Denis is fearless; as he asks the question, his eyes are sparkling.

"As you like—"

"Wait, Master Claude. If you tell Denis that he may do as he pleases, he will take it quite literally."

"Oh— Yes, if I can do whatever I like, then—!"

"......"

Apparently, Aileen's warning has gotten through to him. Claude thinks on it for a little while.

"...If possible, I would like it to be an easy place for the demons to live."

Denis's eyes go perfectly round, and then he folds his arms.

"Demons... Demons, huh? ...Hmm... Is it possible to talk to the demons about this, then?"

"Beelzebuth. Interpret for them."

"Yes, sire."

"You may ask Keith about the finer points. I will be available to make decisions as the need arises. Now, if you'll excuse me."

As he speaks, Claude rises from his throne. Aileen frowns and calls to him.

"Master Claude? Are you feeling unwell?"

"...What do you mean?"

"You are always expressionless, and you never make pointless conversation; in addition, you always conduct yourself as befits your position, so I understand why you would put on a display like this in front of others, but... Aren't you more on edge than usual? The rain seems to be growing steadily worse as well..."

It seems as if it's a sign of Claude's low spirits. She finds it very concerning.

"If something displeases you, do tell me. I'll take appropriate steps to address the issue."

"...There's nothing in particular that needs addressing. However... Let's see. I do have one question."

"What is it?"

"Did you really think Cedric would be happy if you succeeded while trailing a retinue like that?"

She wasn't expecting that question at all, and she looks blank.

Master Cedric? Why are we talking about him now?

It doesn't make any sense. As if he's anticipated Aileen's reaction, Claude speaks before she responds.

"Well, even then, it isn't as though I condone his actions, but..."

"What is it you're trying to say? Speak plainly, please. You aren't Master Cedric, you know."

Aileen's tone is firm, and for a moment, Claude widens his eyes very slightly in surprise. Then his expression turns sober again.

"What is this I've heard about you possibly losing your rank?"

This time, it's Aileen's turn to be startled.

"...Where did you hear about that?"

"As I said earlier, if I try, I can hear any conversation held inside the barrier. You were speaking about it with that man there."

Oops. Acutely aware of the elementary mistake she's made, Aileen looks down in embarrassment.

"Well, I mean, I invited you to a soiree and spoke boldly about how I intended to keep you, and yet I may not be a duke's daughter for much longer. That's mortifying."

"...That was your only reason?"

"What do you mean, 'only'? Master Claude, you have no idea how unstylish commoners are compelled to be!"

Flaring up, Aileen glares at the gorgeous demon king. Claude seems to flinch, but even then, his beauty and elegance are unchanged. She finds it seriously annoying.

"As a commoner, I wouldn't even be able to wear a simple dress like this one! You, Master Claude, would be handsome even in rags or completely naked, so no doubt the idea doesn't bother you, but at any rate!"

"...No, being completely naked would be..."

"Master Claude, now is not the time to point that out."

"The fact that I am armed with a fine dress, cosmetics, and my rank is what enables me to stand tall in your presence now! If I were an ordinary woman, I'd rather die than be at your side! I am able to extend that invitation to you precisely because I am a duke's daughter and can dress myself in fineries! Is that clear?!"

Even after she's said all this in a rush, Claude is silent for a while. Panting, Aileen continues to glare at him.

"...I will keep my promise. No matter your position."

When Claude finally speaks, his red eyes meet Aileen's gaze earnestly.

"Besides, whether you are the daughter of a duke or not, I do not think you yourself would change."

Clichés. The world is hardly ever so convenient or compliant.

However, his words make her heart beat oddly fast. Claude's gaze is suddenly unbearable.

"He's so right. Actually, if you were completely naked, that would be bette— Beelzebuff, wha ezacly ah oo ooin?"

"The king's malice has gathered upon you. I don't really understand why, but as the king wishes, you should die, Keith."

"Merely covering his mouth is fine, Bel... Then if you'll excuse me."

"Wait just a moment. Why were you in a bad mood, then, Master Claude?"

That still hasn't been resolved. However, Claude abruptly smiles.

"Who knows? I'm not so certain myself."

"Wha...?"

Aileen tries to retort, but he's vanished. At the same time, the alabaster throne room also disappears.

"What was that...? What on earth...?"

"No, no, it's fine, isn't it? It looks as though Master Claude's mood has improved."

Keith points toward the sky. It isn't raining anymore; the weather has cleared again.

She doesn't feel quite satisfied, but at any rate, they've completed their formal introductions to Claude. Eager to get down to business, Aileen turns back to the group. All its members are wearing rather odd expressions.

"Now then, let us discuss the work."

"Geez, you change up fast! And actually, about that conversation just now—"

"Don't say it, Young Master Isaac!"

"Who's a 'young master,' Mr. 'I'm a defender of justice'?!"

"From what I hear, if you upset the demon king, he causes whirlwinds and lightning strikes."

Jasper has caught Isaac by the shoulders. Isaac shuts up. Luc murmurs, looking sober.

"Between him and Prince Cedric, I wonder who the better alternative is?"

"...They're hard to compare."

"The demon king seemed like a decent guy, though. He really was pretty, wasn't he? I'd like to make a sculpture of him."

"Never mind that, everyone. We must get to work. I don't have the leeway to squander your time."

Aileen speaks firmly. Shooting glances at one another, everyone reluctantly turns to face her.

"Denis, please renovate the castle in line with Master Claude's wishes. Master Beelzebuth, do interpret for him and the demons."

"I suppose I must. King's orders and all that. Come, child."

"Huh? Child? Maybe I don't look it, but I'm sixteen, you know."

"Jasper, you investigate the misappropriation. Master Keith says he'll assist you."

"...Righto. Thanks for the help, Mr. Attendant."

"Yes, yes, I'm looking forward to it. Let's go bleed 'em dry!"

Keith's eyes are shining, and Jasper's cheeks tense up. Thinking those two will probably be fine if she leaves them to their own devices, Aileen turns to the most difficult hurdle.

"Isaac, Luc, and Quartz. I want the three of you to help me launch my new enterprise."

"A new one, hmm...? I remember the formulas I came up with for soap and things. Why not make the same products? If we improve them, it could work..."

"...We still have a little of the ingredients left."

Isaac speaks before Aileen can.

"Nah, we can't do that. Prince Cedric's a louse, but he's not stupid. Aileen's going to sign her business over to him at the soiree a month and a half from now. I'm willing to bet there's going to be a noncompete clause in there. Even if we make a few improvements, there's a high probability that he'll use it to justify his grievances and either shut the new business down or take it away again. That means if we're doing this, we need something completely different. We need to develop products that nobody can call medicines. So what is it you want to make?"

He really is sharp. Aileen smiles.

"I had something I wanted to try already. Cosmetics."

"Cosmetics?"

"The women of the nobility positively squander money on their own beauty. Cosmetics are practically vital necessities for noblewomen. We'll exploit that. There's a risk that it will lower my reputation with the aristocracy, so I'd avoided it thus far, but..."

When selling to nobles, the fact that the customers you court are members of the nobility makes it easy for business problems to become political ones. It was a proposal that she'd voluntarily shelved out of consideration for Prince Cedric's reputation, so that she'd have as few political enemies as possible.

Even so, both her brothers and her father had initially considered the idea promising and said it had potential.

"...It's worth doing. I'm in. Luc, Quartz? What about you?"

Folding his arms, Isaac turns to the other two, who would be central players in the development work.

"You can say that, but I'm not really seeing it. I understand that medicines won't do, but..."

"Think of it this way, Luc: Cosmetics are medicines that beautify women's skin."

Up until just a little while ago, women in this world had smeared beeswax on their faces, then dusted and dabbed face powder over it, almost as if they were painting pictures.

However, makeup isn't the same as paint. Cosmetics are pharmaceuticals designed to be used on skin. In her previous life, her skin was as fragile as the rest of her, and in the end, she turned to homemade alternatives. As a result, she's familiar with the basics.

Right now, in this world, cosmetics are still simple paints. They haven't yet entered the realm of scientific development.

"Visualize treating a skin disorder. When your hands get rough, you apply a salve to keep them from getting chapped, correct? It's the same concept."

"...I see. I think I understand. I'll give it a try... What about you, Quartz?"

"...The basic component of a cosmetic solution must be water. The sort that makes your hands smooth when you wash them... Like sponge gourd water, maybe?"

"Yes, that's it exactly!"

She thinks she's heard of something like that before.

That being said, I really don't know how we'd go about collecting deep-sea water or hyaluronic acid!

Eventually, she'd like someone to develop them...although it seems likely it would take quite a long time before that day ever comes.

"Fundamentally, it's about softness and moisture retention. Water and fragrance... You must have essential oils, correct? We'll mix those in. Oh, and perhaps we could sell fragrances as well? No one's tried aromatherapy massages around here, have they?"

"Aroma...? What's that?"

"I'll explain later. Have those ready before the soiree. I'll use them myself, and if Master Claude is on my arm, the reputation of both should improve handsomely."

"A walking advertisement, huh? Yeah, the demon king is real good-looking."

"He *is*! And so let's at least raise me to a level where I won't lose when he's standing beside me."

Aileen sounds so desperate that Isaac pulls back a bit.

"What, that's your motive here?!"

"Yes, is there a problem?! I am confident they'll sell. It's a matter of life and death for noblewomen!"

"You're quite lovely as it is, Lady Aileen."

"...The demon king basically isn't human. It's better not to compete with..."

"Demon king or human, when a man has skin and hair that beautiful, it's humiliating to a lady all by itself! What in the world *is* that? As a woman, I refuse to lose!"

"...I see, yeah. This'll be lucrative."

Isaac mutters quietly, and the others nod, looking grave.

Unintentionally, simply by speaking her own mind, Aileen has convinced them that her new enterprise is viable.

"Yes! This is it, this scent! I'm so glad you've managed to extract it...!"

The fragrance of lavender closely matches her memories from her previous life, and Aileen smiles, satisfied. Luc looks at Denis.

"It's thanks to the steam distiller you made, Denis."

"I'd like rosemary as well. I'm quite fond of that scent."

"It does have a nice fragrance, but... In that case, should we do chamomile too, then?"

"Yes, I think so. I'd also like to make fruit blends. Orange and lemon. Then let's make several basic cosmetic solutions that have different effects. We'll give them a high-rarity value and set expensive prices."

"Here's a timely present from me, then."

Isaac drops a large envelope stuffed with documents into Luc's hands.

"I pulled together examples of clinical situations in which herbs and essential oils were used and displayed effects. That, and popular folk rumors."

"Lavender essential oil is effective on burns... The black plague was prevented with herbs? Is this true?"

As Luc flips through the papers, Quartz peeks in at them from beside him.

"They used thyme, sage, mint, and... All of these are highly antibacterial. They pickled them in vinegar, so they called it 'herb vinegar,' hmm? In that case, you could anticipate them having strong antibacterial properties..."

"In other words, it was an antiseptic? ...Do you think we could distribute this among the masses? It looks as though the commoners were the ones who discovered its use in the first place..."

"If we can figure out a way to sell it so that it doesn't look like medicine."

Isaac is wearing a sly smile. Aileen nods.

"We'll work on that angle, but later. First, we need capital. There's the cosmetic solution, and I'd also like to use this in bath salts and soaps. If you find anything else, report it right away, please."

"Understood. This forest certainly is amazing."

"There are plants I've never even seen before—maybe because they've adapted to suit the demons' environment."

"However, harvesting them without affecting the demons' ecosystem is vital. If we break that rule, Master Claude will be angry."

Quartz nods. He's always very careful with plants, so it may not even have been necessary to warn him about that.

"And then the castle renovations. Denis, how are those progressing?"

"Very well! I really wasn't sure how it was going to go at first, but I hardly ever get to make houses for demons, and at this point, I'm having so much fun, I can barely contain myself! I think this kitchen came out well, don't you?!"

Beaming, Denis spreads his arms wide.

On the demons' request, the very first place they finished was this kitchen, where Aileen and the others have gathered. Since there are no other good places for their meetings, they're holding them at the long table that would ordinarily have been the servants' dining table.

Because Keith said they didn't anticipate ever having guests, the room is on the small side for a castle kitchen. However, the layout is just right, and it's been built so that the location of the fireplace, the food storage, and even the back door that leads outside have all been conveniently placed.

"Except what we're doing is brewing grasses and flowers."

"Still, if we get all the ingredients, Lady Aileen can make sweets here, too."

"I don't have that kind of time. There's still one big problem left."

"What?! Make cookies, girl!"

A crow with a bow tie flits out of the shadow behind her. More demons swarm and follow them, congregating at Aileen's feet and on top of her head.

"Almond is me! Cake should be strawberry!"

"Gimme pie..."

"Tart, I know not. I eat."

She doesn't turn around, but blue veins pop up on her temples.

"Refrain from using my shadow as a convenient entrance, would you...? Go back. Right this instant!"

"Cookies! Cookies!"

"Cake! Cake!"

"Don't chant at me! You were the ones who devoured all the sweets I had in my room the other day while I was sleeping, wasn't it?!"

"It's your fault! You didn't bring enough!"

This is an incredible show of unjustified defiance. However, it's a horde against one, and even the other demons begin to clamor.

"If you don't make, we'll take all the sugar and get in the way!"

"We won't let you take other plants, either! We'll teach you nothing!"

"Except Denis! The roof keeps rain out now! He's a good!"

"For goodness' sake, I'll make them and listen to you once I'm finished working, so just wait!"

Grabbing the flying crow with her bare hands, she tries to shove them back into the opening in her shadow.

However, the crow flaps, impudently resisting.

"Tyrant, tyrant! We'll tell the demon king on you!"

"That's my line. I've told you for the last time, I'm working!"

"...Don't get in her way."

At the sound of the quiet voice, the demons' commotion stops dead.

"Also, even if it's through that shadow, don't venture outside the barrier carelessly."

"Understood, understood!"

"You said that the other day, too, and then you came to snack— Stop right there! Are you trying to flee?!"

Watching the demons dive into her shadow and disappear one after another, Aileen stamps her feet in frustration. With no other recourse, she glares at Claude, who's standing in the doorway with Keith.

"Master Claude, give the demons a firmer warning, if you would. They're constantly coming to my room to pester me for sweets, particularly those crows!"

"I believe you were collecting information regarding the forest in exchange for those sweets."

"That is a completely different matter! Perhaps I'll dose them with a numbing agent again…!"

"If you do, they may stop telling you where delicious berries grow."

Keith wears a meaningful smile. Aileen folds her arms and sighs.

"…I will give them their just rewards, but manners are important. Do scold them properly, Master Claude. If demons are sighted at the mansion of Duke d'Autriche, there will be an uproar."

"The demons think you will handle it somehow for them."

"And as I am telling you, that isn't—!"

"Come, come, enough talk of educational policies for the demons. We've managed to acquire capital, so I've arrived to report in. I tell you, we resolved that in no time at all. Jasper is a brilliant fellow!"

Taking advantage of the fact that Jasper has an urgent deadline for an article and isn't here, Keith makes a slapdash report. She gives him a cold look.

"Jasper was afraid of you, you know. He said you produced proof in no time at all. Almost as if you'd had it on hand already."

"Oh, no, that was mere coincidence."

"Not only that, but you also provided him with a different corruption lead, and what's more, you refused to tell him the name of the culprit behind the original misappropriation. What are you playing at?"

"Well, I mean, an article about how the demon king had no living expenses would make us look preposterous, wouldn't it?"

The pile of lavender on the table all begins to wilt at once. Right away, Denis shouts:

"Oh— The demon king's hurt!"

"That's how it is, so please rest easy and apply yourselves to your tasks, everyone. I'll put my very best efforts into preparing for the soiree! I'll dress Master Claude in his finest, so be sure he doesn't outshine you, Miss Aileen!"

Keith is smirking, quite obviously enjoying the situation. Aileen fights back with a ladylike smile.

"Yes, I'll do my best."

"Wow, we'll be looking forward to that. Won't we, Master Claude?!"

Even she is startled by how much hearing that name unsettles her. However, thanks to her ironclad practiced smile, which she honed to perfection in preparation for becoming empress, she manages not to show it. As naturally as possible, she turns her gaze on Claude.

However, although his features are as lovely as ever, Claude has frozen up.

"......"

This really ought to have been small talk, and yet the silence is terribly heavy. *I'm begging you, say something, anything.* Just as her smile seems about to stiffen up, Claude moves his lips, as if in a gasp.

"...Not particularly."

That's all he says, and then he abruptly averts his face and vanishes.

An odd silence hangs in the kitchen. Aileen, now calm, murmurs softly.

"...Does he mean that dressing up won't change me particularly...? All right, everyone! We will complete this cosmetic solution and silence Master Claude, no matter what it takes!"

"Huh...? That's your takeaway, Miss Aileen? The demon king's pure heart is working against him!"

"That's too bad. It looks like she doesn't even get why she's so irritated."

Keith and Isaac are rather exasperated. Smacking her hands down onto the long table, Aileen breaks up the mood.

"Go on, back to work! There's only a month left until the soiree!"

"Hey, the lavender's back to normal."

At Denis's murmur, everyone shrugs. However, Aileen is still upset, and she doesn't see what's fairly obvious to everyone else.

Before long, the trial version of the cosmetic solution is complete. When they test it with women of the upper classes—carefully selected by Isaac, with due consideration given to confidentiality—it is supremely well-received. There's plenty of potential here.

The problem is how to sell it.

Even if I attempt to sell it personally, my name alone might get me turned away at the gate. Before, I'd assumed the d'Autriche name would be enough to buy trust, so I didn't give much thought to advertising, but at this point...

She scans the list of people who are scheduled to attend the soiree; she's had Jasper check into the event for her. This will be the first soiree the crown prince will be hosting, and the list is studded with the names of great aristocrats. If she plays her cards well here, she'll be on the right track.

We've created good products. If we can convince people to use them, they're sure to be a success. The problem is how to go about doing it. Should I humble myself and ask? No, if I did that, they'd only take advantage of me...

She hears a rustle. Aileen is sitting at the desk in her own room, holding a quill pen, and she speaks without turning around.

"I'll tell Master Claude on you."

"......"

"That's Almond, isn't it? I swear, you never learn— Oh."

As Aileen turns to look, her eyes widen. The individual standing there is not a crow demon with a bow tie, but Beelzebuth.

...*That's right. He is a demon, isn't he? I suppose he can use my shadow as well.*

She thinks something slightly foolish.

Sneaking into a lady's room in the middle of the night... Demon or not, since he looks like a young man, it's an unforgivable deed. However, there's simply no chance that he would do so for any ordinary reason, and so confusion wins out.

"...Girl. I have a request."

"Goodness, what's brought this on?"

She tilts her head in genuine bewilderment, not sarcasm, and the worried wrinkles between Beelzebuth's eyes deepen.

"I would prefer not to ask, either. However, the boy told me that you were the one for the job."

"Do you mean Denis? Honestly, I'm not a handyman. But very well. Out with it."

"...The king is going to attend a soiree, isn't he? I would like to go with him."

Aileen blinks emphatically. Beelzebuth heaves a deep sigh.

"I know that Keith is accompanying him. However, if he is the only one there, I'll worry."

"Even if you do attend with him, all retainers may do is stand in the corner, you know."

"Still... This soiree will be a gathering of the humans who

drove the king away. To him, it will be a battlefield. The king is strong. He will not lose."

With eyes that hold unwavering trust, Beelzebuth goes on.

"However, he may be hurt."

"......"

"In order to avoid embarrassing the king at this soiree, I hear I will need the power known as 'manners.' I would like to acquire this power."

So that I may at least be by his side.

There is an intense appeal in his eyes, and Aileen responds with a wry smile. *I can't turn this down.*

"All right."

"Will you grant me the power of manners?"

"Yes, I will grant it to you. There's still a month left. To begin with, I will make sure you look the part. After all, you are Master Claude's right-hand man and his knight."

Beelzebuth looks thrilled. That innocence is genuine.

"Master Claude is fortunate... More than anything, he is curious."

Beelzebuth cocks his head in a show of confusion. His pure, perplexed expression stirs up such feelings of wonder and jealousy that she quietly reveals what's in her heart.

"He protects the demons and also saves humans... It makes me wonder what sort of person he really is."

"He is the demon king."

"Yes. That may be the very definition of a demon king. It's dangerous to approach him, and it's impossible to know what may happen. However, for that very reason, no one can ignore him... Wait, that's it!"

It's truly a divine revelation. Rising to her feet, she takes another look at the list of soiree guests.

"We should target this one, and this one... If I recall, these two get along badly; we'll use that...!"

"Hey, girl. I want you to give me manners quickly."

"Yes, of course. You will have to be a knight who'll make young noblewomen's hearts race."

This should work. Wearing a corrupt merchant's smirk, Aileen promptly turns to face Beelzebuth.

Then, lightly crossing her arms, she gives him an elegant smile.

"And so first, kneel to me."

"...Is it your fault Beelzebuth's been strange lately?"

Aileen is standing on the castle's brand-new terrace, surveying the scene below, when a voice calls down to her. She looks up.

Directly below, Denis is barking instructions at the craftsmen who are running around working on the renovations. However, no one seems startled by the demon king floating in midair.

It's already a familiar sight to them.

"Strange? He's grown knightlier recently, hasn't he?"

"He gave me an endless demonstration of proper salutations..."

"Do check on that for him, at least. There's a week left before the soiree. He's working very hard, Master Claude, simply because he wants to be there with you."

Looking as if he has mixed feelings about that, Claude descends to the terrace. The young fenrir, who was sitting at Aileen's feet, stands up and yields their spot to him. Standing beside Aileen, Claude gazes from the terrace at the surrounding lands.

"I also hear you've been luring the demons to do more of your bidding, using sweets."

"I haven't forced them. Or do I need your permission for every little thing, Master Claude?"

"No... They seem to be enjoying themselves as well, so it's fine."

Cheerful voices reach them from down below. She can see a flock of crows carrying baskets around their necks. There's also a wolfman who sets up a heavy beam of timber as if it weighs next to nothing, then holds it in place.

As Claude watches them, he looks vaguely happy. Even though it's winter, the wind blowing across the terrace feels gentle.

"The demons tell me that if they help with the construction, the crafters will build houses for them, too."

"Yes. Demons have strength that humans don't possess. Denis said he can't leave the finer tasks to them, but when it comes to physical labor and transportation, they're very reliable."

Thanks to that, the castle restorations are progressing at more than double the usual speed. Denis had finally said, *"I'll pay, so could you come and work for me?"*

In response, every demon expressed interest, as long as the demon king granted them permission.

"I'm sure they'll do fine work, even outside the barrier. Would you have them become members of my trading company? Their duties will consist mainly of disaster recovery. You can be an executive, Master Claude, and we shall work to improve the demons' image."

"I will take it under consideration."

Possibly because he thinks refusing would be pointless in any case, he gives her a diplomatic answer. Although she's asked him, Aileen can't imagine Claude becoming her subordinate, so she backs down and changes the subject.

"Master Claude, the territory you govern—the demons' land—is surprisingly vast."

"...Yes. At first, it truly was only this abandoned castle and the forest, but..."

Claude gazes into the distance.

"Things are calm now, but long ago, demons who had been chased from their homes by humans often came here. After a while, it grew cramped, and soon there was not enough room for all the demons to live comfortably or food for them to eat."

"A demon refugee problem—I see. How did you handle it?"

"Keith purchased an adjacent plot of land. At the time, it was the territory of a count, I think."

Casually, Claude points beyond the forest.

"As you go to the north, the weather becomes harsher, and the land poorer. Not only that, but it also shares a border with the demon king's forest. While it is close to the imperial capital, it must not have been worth much. I hear he was able to purchase it rather cheaply."

"But the other party must have had his honor as titled nobility to consider. I imagine the negotiations must have been difficult... Master Keith really is quite capable, isn't he?"

"Yes. I trust him in all things."

His face is as expressionless as ever, but she can tell he means that. Aileen feels a prickling pain deep in her chest.

"I envy Master Keith."

"You do? Why?"

"Master Claude. Empresses are subjects as well... I feel my failure to win Master Cedric's trust was my oversight as his attendant."

A strong wind blows, rolling back the leaves of the trees. At her feet, the young fenrir gives a soft cry.

"Now that I think about it, there were signs. I was always the one who went to see him. I never received a present from him. He insisted on leaving the business in my hands... My, you know, things may not be that different now."

As she thinks about that, without warning, Claude drapes his cloak over her head.

In the midst of the whistling, blustering wind, he murmurs:

"You must be cold. Let's go in."

"Oh, thank you very much... Um, Master Claude? This wind— Or rather, I believe I see a whirlwind over there..."

"I am not like Cedric."

Oh, so that's why he's in a bad mood.

Understanding, Aileen smiles beneath that abruptly ominous sky.

"I know that. You will come to the soiree as promised, won't you, Master Claude?"

"...Has he ever broken an appointment with you?"

"Yes, at last year's school festival."

Cedric didn't appear, and Aileen had been left waiting by herself. If things had gone according to the game, Cedric had been enjoying his own private ball on the roof, all alone with Lilia, under the stars.

"Even if something happens and I am unable to attend, I will explain myself properly."

Claude doesn't make a superficial promise that he'll attend without fail, and that certainly does make him unlike Cedric.

Aileen feels reassured, and she nods.

"However, no matter your reasons, if you fail to show up, I will require appropriate compensation from you."

"For example…?"

"Marry me."

She expects him to be annoyed, but instead, he falls to thinking, his face serious. Wrapped in Claude's cloak, Aileen blinks at him.

"My, have you finally resigned yourself?"

"…If you cry and beg me, I could consider it."

"Why do you want to make me cry so very badly?!"

"I suspect it's because you have the sort of personality that makes people want to take you down a peg, Miss Aileen."

Keith's voice issues from the interior of the terrace. When she looks, it isn't just Keith; Jasper is there, too, a peculiar expression on his face.

"True, Miss Aileen is the type of woman you want to bring to tears. I guess you'd call it men's baser nature."

"If that is the sort of creatures men are, eradicate them at once!"

"What do you two need? Are you voyeurs?"

"The mood there was very good, and I'm teeeerribly sorry, but… Jasper's brought us some rather unfavorable news."

He shoots the other man a glance. Jasper grasps the edge of his beret.

"Miss, there's a rumor that you are conspiring with demons and are targeting Lady Lilia's life. Marcus is the source."

"In that case, it must have its origins in the recent commotion at the academy."

At Aileen's feet, the young fenrir blinks. Claude frowns, his forehead creasing.

"Marcus? Who is that, Keith?"

"I heard you'd beaten him hollow, but you don't even remember him, milord. I'd expect no less of you."

"...Was there a person like that?"

Not only does Marcus exist, but Claude himself also knocked him down in front of Lilia.

Heavens, I almost feel a little sorry for him.

To think he didn't even see him. The demon king is cold-blooded indeed.

Jasper clears his throat pointedly.

"W-well, differences in perception aside, it sounds as though Lady Lilia has gotten multiple threatening letters. It's the usual drivel: 'You're not fit to be Master Cedric's fiancée, step down, or else'—that sort of thing. Well, for a woman set on marrying a prince, it's basically a rite of passage."

"Very true. But why am I supposed to be the culprit?"

"I hear some of the letters were signed *Aileen Lauren d'Autriche*. On top of that, they were written on this high-quality scented stationery that noblewomen use. Master Cedric is taking the whole incident pretty seriously, and he's making a fuss about it."

As she tries to laugh, pain shoots through her temples. Flickering, a scene from the game rises in her mind's eye.

Threats... That's right, the heroine did receive those. The kidnapping incident was the result... In the game, the letters were sent by...

The mastermind behind the kidnapping, and the villainess who hoped to get back together with Cedric: Aileen Lauren d'Autriche.

"...That's not even funny. If I were going to send threatening letters to anyone, I'd write, *Don't ever get involved with me again. Come near me, and I'll kill you*, and send them to Master Cedric."

"Well, we believe you, but the general public will be harder to convince. In particular, the nobles who think Prime Minister d'Autriche is an eyesore couldn't ask for better ammunition."

Is someone attempting to entrap her? At first glance, the events seem to be following exactly what happened in the game...

However, in the game, Aileen's name hadn't been on the letters. Considering that juvenile touch, this doesn't actually seem all that similar.

"Since the letters arrived, Lady Lilia's personal guard has been strengthened, and even then, another letter in your name got through. There's a rumor that it's likely the work of demons..."

"Oh, and that brings us back to my colluding with demons."

Instead of nodding, Jasper sighs.

"Since they're chalking it all up to the work of demons, they haven't even conducted a proper investigation. Lady Lilia's scared and crying, while Master Cedric's flying into fits of rage. It's tiresome over there."

"Goodness, to think she'd be frightened of mere threatening letters. I've gotten so many of those at once that I've tossed them all into the fire and then boiled some water, you know."

"That doesn't seem like the most normal reaction, either!"

"In any case, there's very little time left before the soiree. Let's mark the criminal out right from the start and investigate."

"Look, that's easy to say, but..."

"Threatening letters that slip through the eyes of a guard detail so strict that it seems they could only be from the work of demons? The culprit is bound to be an insider, correct?"

Aileen smiles fearlessly, and Jasper scratches his head.

"The largest purveyor of stationery for noblewomen is the trading company Isaac's family runs. Call Isaac later, would you?

And then... Almond, can you hear me? If you can, come out, please. I'll reward you, of course."

"What?!"

A demon flies out of the shadow that stretches across the terrace, and Jasper flinches, startled. The crow with the bow tie lands on the terrace balustrade. Keith mutters, sounding as if he has mixed feelings about this.

"So you can use that shadow to summon demons, hmm...?"

"A job! Sounds fun! Pay me with apple pie!"

"I'll throw in cake as well. Your job is to bring back the royal castle's rubbish."

"Easy! Leave it to me!"

"No."

Claude is the one who's objected. Naturally, Almond promptly changes his tune.

"Can't be done! I refuse!"

"I simply want him to pretend he's an ordinary crow and bring back garbage—documents—from the palace. It won't be dangerous."

"However, the servants who throw the garbage away will see him. There may be traps, too."

"—Master Claude. I've been meaning to say this for quite some time: You coddle the demons too much."

"My power doesn't extend beyond the barrier. This is a natural safety measure."

"Keeping them shut away because it's dangerous outside? That's no solution. Parents who don't teach their children how to handle knives because of the potential dangers are merely fools. You should allow the demons to acquire worldly wisdom as well.

After all, it isn't as if you can protect everything and everyone by yourself."

She leans in, pushing her face up toward Claude's. Claude is expressionless, but he flinches very slightly and retreats.

"Almond, what about you? Do you want to do the job? Or would you rather not?"

"For me, the demon king's orders take top priority."

"That wasn't an order just now. It was only a restriction."

The crow's appropriately almond-shaped eyes dart around. He seems to be thinking, and he glances restlessly from Claude to Aileen and back again.

Finally, as if she's outlasted Claude, the demon king exhales.

"...You may do as you wish. However, if you feel it's danger-ous, return immediately. That is an order."

Almond bobs his head, bow tie and all. Then Claude turns his cold eyes on Aileen.

"If anything happens, I will never allow humans to set foot inside this castle or the forest ever again."

"Before you do, I'll personally thrash any human who's responsible. I think Almond is precious as well— Why is everyone looking at me like that?"

Never mind Claude; even Almond looks stunned, his beak hang-ing open. Jasper folds his arms before adjusting the beret on his head.

"Probably because of all the things you usually say and do. Your love is hard to understand, Miss Aileen."

"When I am taking some of my precious time to entrust some-one with a job, my affection for them is quite strong, you know."

The others look as if they want to say, *Case in point...*, but she flatly ignores them.

"Almond. As Master Claude says, if you think it's dangerous, flee immediately. On top of that, always act in groups. Both keeping an eye on the rubbish and bringing it back will be a process. I leave the decision of which companion will bear which role to you."

"I decide."

"That's right. You're the captain."

Almond puffs up all his plumage, and his eyes glitter. Then he cleverly bends one wing in a sharp salute.

"Aye aye, sir!"

"My. Where did you learn to salute?"

"From Isaac! Saloot, roger!"

There are quite a few mistakes in there, but apparently, this pose has tickled his fancy. The way he salutes with his wing and puffs out his feathery chest is adorable in a very undemonic way, and rather charming.

Jasper also gives him a good, hard look, then whistles.

"That's an air force salute. Good, very good. You are the demon king's air wing, after all."

"...In that case, as their commanding officer, it's my job to keep my subordinates alive."

Aileen smiles smugly. Claude glances at her before quietly asking her a question.

"Is there anything I can do?"

Everyone stares at him. Aileen freezes up for a few seconds too, her eyes wide.

Out of all of them, only Claude looks at his own feet.

"It's strange. My desire to make you cry hasn't changed, but..."

"No, please do change that!"

"Sometimes, I begin wanting to spoil you utterly rotten."

And again, why do words that should sound sweet veer off in a suspicious direction?

Whatever happened to the "aloof demon king" setting?!

She really wishes he wouldn't turn a bracing afternoon into an obscene honeymoon with a lilting atmosphere of depravity. Backing away, Aileen gives him a tense smile.

"Y-you jest too much... Wait, where has everyone gone?!"

"They scattered like rabbits."

Even Almond and the young fenrir have vanished. She feels as if she's a sacrifice who's been offered to the demon king. Putting a hand to her forehead, Aileen draws a deep breath.

Calm down, be calm... The important thing is— Yes, the fact that Master Claude seems willing to do you a favor! Now is the time to present him with a formal marriage contract or—

And yet for some reason, she can't bring herself to say it. She has the feeling that she'll end up ruined for life.

"In that case—at the soiree, please be a more dashing escort than any other gentleman... More than Master Cedric."

After she thinks and thinks, the wish that comes out is a foolish one. Once she's said it, she feels like dropping her head into her hands.

I should at least have asked him to develop collagen! Or no, is that wrong, too?! Aaaaaah, there, see? Judging from that look he's giving me, Master Claude must be thinking, What on earth is wrong with this woman?

For some inexplicable reason, even though she has so many wishes that she can't count them all, that was the only one she could manage. She's so embarrassed that she wants to run away, but Claude averts his eyes first.

"You really are formidable."

"Huh...?"

"I promise."

Before she can ask him *Promise what?* Claude launches himself from the terrace and descends to the ground.

Remembering what the promise consists of, Aileen puts her hands to her cheeks, which have belatedly grown hot.

—On the morning of the soiree, sitting by her pillow, she discovers a gown, shoes, and a complete set of accessories, addressed to her and signed by Claude Jeane Ellmeyer.

She'd taken steps against nearly everything that worried her. She feels confident that she could win. She is emotionally prepared.

...For everything except that impossible present on the morning of the soiree.

"Very fetching, Aileen. I hardly recognized you."

"Do you really, truly mean that, Father?"

Aileen turns around, her eyes intense. Rudolph blinks at her.

"Does it suit me? I'm not being shown up by my own dress, am I? Me, of all people!"

"Wh-what's the matter? This isn't like you. Even when you were making your society debut, you never said anything like that. Don't tell me you're frightened you might lose to Lady Lilia."

"Never mind a bit player like her; I'm up against the world's most bewitching demon! My hair and makeup should be perfect, but even so, I worry!"

She's on edge. She's checked herself in the mirror over and over, so many times that the servants finally dragged her away and bundled her into the carriage, and yet she still hasn't checked enough.

Maybe I should have chosen a slightly more mature red for my lipstick. Would it have been better to do my hair up tightly?

But she no longer has time or a mirror. Her father takes her hand, leading her, and she steps onto the shining marble floor of the evening's venue.

For a moment, silence spreads through the room.

With its bustle and extravagant use of glossy-white silk, her dress looks as pure as a bride's at first glance.

However, the glimpses of elaborate black lace, the embroidery in gold thread, and the black rose accents that match her hair ornament all take the impression—which might otherwise have seemed too youthful—and sharpen it into something alluring.

As solitary colors, both white and black would be frowned on at a soiree unless there's a good reason for them. However, this dress, with its combination of white and black shot through with what seems like gold filigree, draws people's eyes like a starry sky. Some gazes are critical, while others are curious, a mixture of criticism and envy. It's the mood that's invariably in the air just before a new fashion trend takes off.

Not only that, but when the one wearing that dress is also *the* Aileen Lauren d'Autriche, well...

Instead of her usual haughty smile, her eyes are downcast and rather melancholy. The shadows cast by her long lashes accentuate the paleness of her skin. Her full lips are like succulent fruit, and with every step she takes, the sophisticated scent of black roses wafts around her.

No matter how disgraced she may be, she is undeniably beautiful, down to each strand of her hair.

Aileen herself doesn't register how the room is receiving her, however.

Master Claude chose this dress, didn't he? I was supposed to wear it here, wasn't I? It does suit me, doesn't it? He gave it to me because it suits me, right?!

Her cheeks flush faintly. When she blinks, her eyes damp, she makes eye contact with a young nobleman who's gazing at her, captivated, as if he's feebleminded. On reflex, Aileen smiles at him lightly.

"...You've changed a bit, haven't you? At this point, I suspect Prince Cedric would fall for you all over again."

"What? What are you saying, Father? I'd turn him down even if it killed me."

"I see... I thought it might be a viable move, you know. We would have been able to milk him for this and that."

Her father chuckles, but his eyes are half-serious.

"That said, no doubt you'd be too much for the average man. All right, this is as far as I go, my dear. I'll be looking forward to hearing about your exploits."

He gives her a thumbs-up. His complexion is rosy. In other words, there's probably a tricky development or two waiting in the wings.

Well, it would be dull if we won too easily, I suppose— My.

Isaac approaches her. Tonight, his hair is neatly combed, and he's dressed like a proper young aristocrat. No one speaks to him, but he knows he's the center of attention.

Pausing on his way past her, Isaac gives a quiet report.

"It's a roaring success. This reputation is just what we were aiming for."

"I see."

"—I did think that *someone* would have a connection to the Oberon Trading Firm!"

That name promptly jumps out at her, and she focuses her ears, listening in.

"What is the meaning of this? How can I not have received one? Count Wames's daughter did!"

"It's rumored that they're sent only to select young ladies. As a result, you-know-who is furious."

"I hear it was by her pillow when she woke. The servants say none of them know anything about it. It's like magic! I confess just hearing about it thrilled me."

"Using it feels marvelous. My skin is in such wonderful condition; I can't imagine using anything else anymore."

"Oh no! I thought it was suspicious and threw it away. What shall I do? Isn't there anywhere one can get ahold of it?"

"I heard there were some who received not only a cosmetic solution but also facial soap..."

"The trial products are nearly gone already. I thought at this soiree, someone might know, but—"

"My wife wants some, and she refuses to stop going on and on about it. Now I'm stumped; to think no one knows anything..."

Involuntarily, Aileen breaks into a smile. When she covertly extends a hand toward Isaac, he smacks it lightly in celebration.

"Now, as planned, I'll go spread a rumor that the d'Autriche duchy has a connection to the company."

"Please do."

"Also, the latest news from the guy-and-crows team: First off, the culprit behind the threatening letters is Lilia. She's staging it herself."

That's the spirit, she thinks.

It would have been dull if the woman who'd driven her from her position as fiancée was simply an ordinary woman.

"I see. The pattern on the stationery matched, then. Master Cedric isn't in on it?"

"It doesn't appear so. I've got the proof with me. If you need it, signal me— There is some bad news, though."

"What might that be?"

"Lady Lilia's been missing since this morning. I hear Prince Cedric dispatched a band of apprentice knights, led by Marcus, toward the demon king's forest."

In spite of herself, Aileen turns to look at him, but Isaac keeps speaking to her obliquely.

"Until Lady Lilia is found, I'm told the demon king won't be coming."

"Master Claude— And the demons? Don't tell me they're under attack."

"Calm down; you know there's no way they'd get the demon king easily. Besides, there's that nonaggression pact. The demon king asked me for a favor. Or actually, Almond did; he brought me a message from him this morning."

"This morning?"

If he'd been able to send her a dress, why hadn't he sent word? Aileen frowns, and Isaac looks her straight in the eye.

"He said, 'Until I arrive, take care of Aileen.'"

Of Aileen's companions, the only one who's able to openly attend the soiree is Isaac.

Isaac fixes her with a determined look.

"You can do this, right? After all, you're the woman he and I both put our trust in."

She pulls her chin in tight so that her gaze won't fall. She looks straight ahead, donning a dauntless smile.

"You have groundwork to lay for the matter with Master Claude, don't you? I'll be fine; you take care of that."

"Right— If they'd demoted you to commoner, I would have taken you, you know."

"Make you my husband? I'd never do something so wasteful."

"Ha, fair."

Exchanging a light high five, they walk past each other. Immediately afterward, Cedric appears on the platform, his face grim. Lilia isn't beside him.

If this goes on, Aileen will be named the kidnapper, just as she was in the game. However, she doesn't panic.

Overturning this is precisely how I'll win. Don't underestimate me.

The first time her engagement was broken, she lost. The second time, victory will be hers.

"Arrest Aileen Lauren d'Autriche."

As Cedric issues his order, the guards surround her. Even so, she wears an elegant smile.

The human Beelzebuth has dragged in is dressed in a charming outfit. Her hair looks soft, and her face is sweet. Her full lips and large eyes are pretty.

So this is the woman Cedric chose, is she? Discarding Aileen…

That's the Claude's first impression as he looks down at her from his throne, chin braced on his hand. The renovations on the marble throne room have just been completed. In that room, surrounded by demons, the girl blinks uneasily.

"Thank you for showing me the way… Oh—I'm Lilia

Reinoise. And you are the demon king, aren't you...? Oh, good. Do you remember me?"

Recrossing his long legs, Claude asks only about what concerns him.

"How did you get through the barrier without my knowledge?"

"Huh? What do you mean?"

The girl looks straight into his red eyes. He narrows them as he returns her gaze. There's no fear there.

Her resistance to magic is strong... Does she have a connection to the Maid of the Sacred Sword?

That's why she managed to cross the forest barrier. Claude is convinced. Beelzebuth watches him, looking as if he wants to say something. Sighing, Claude rises to his feet.

"Well, no matter. I will send you home."

"Huh...? Um, please wait! Y-you're angry, aren't you? Because Marcus did something rude to you the other day!"

"I'm not interested in what you have to say."

"I've been thinking I ought to apologize, all this time. And also, I'd like you to make up with Cedric...!"

When he frowns, Lilia stands up, clasping her hands in front of her chest.

"I've heard. You two have always been raised apart... Cedric was concerned. You're surrounded by demons, and even so, you're fulfilling your duty as prince and preventing them from going to war with the humans— This whole situation is just so tragic. All the other humans leave everything to you; it's awful of them. I feel bad for you, having to be all alone..."

"I respect your strength."

Words that are the complete opposite of the ones he's hearing now rise in his mind. What would he have thought if he'd heard this girl's words first?

Beelzebuth is about to say something, but Claude stops him with a glance, then speaks.

"This forest is currently surrounded by the soldiers Cedric has dispatched."

"It's a mistake. Both Marcus and Cedric are kind, so they're worried about me... There's the matter of the threatening letters, too; they've simply acted prematurely."

"You mean *you're* causing them to act prematurely. It was you who wrote those letters, after all."

Lilia widens her large eyes, and she falls still. After that, she lets her shoulders fall.

"...So you knew. I do feel bad about that. Even I felt ashamed... but it was the only way to stop Lady Aileen."

"Stop her?"

"I wanted to tell you that we've seen through Lady Aileen's scheme. I could tell at a glance that you were a kind person, but careless contact between humans and demons can touch off conflict, you know? Why, just the other day, you and Marcus had a confrontation."

At this very moment, the one who's carelessly making contact and creating an excuse to break the nonaggression pact is none other than this girl before him, but Claude stays silent and listens.

"And so before Lady Aileen committed a crime, I ran away on my own. Cedric and Marcus are brilliant, after all; they would have caught her. Those three are childhood friends, you see. It would be sad if they had a falling-out."

"......"

"If I run away during a situation I arbitrarily set up, Lady Aileen won't be charged with a crime. I'll explain it to everyone properly later. I'm sure they'll understand."

I imagine they will, Claude thinks coldly. No doubt the idiots around her would be moved by the fact that kind Lilia had lied in order to shield Aileen from her supposed crime.

Then Aileen would be treated as a criminal that they simply didn't have enough proof to convict—or rather, more importantly…

"You speak as if Aileen harming you is a fundamental given."

"…The thing is, Lady Aileen really did love Cedric."

It's only natural that she'd resent me. Lilia looks meek and troubled as she leaves the thought unspoken.

She doesn't even realize how arrogant that is.

"Besides, I just couldn't leave you on your own. I wanted to see you and talk with you one more time."

Lilia's cheeks flush faintly. She looks up at him softly.

In that moment, Claude's displeasure soars past its upper limit.

A sudden gust of wind kicks up. The storm whips around the throne room, punctuated with loud peals of laughter as the attending demons cover their ears and huddle together. It looks as though it's all Lilia can do to stay on her feet. However, even as she covers her ears, she raises her voice. Her grit is admirable.

"I-I'm sorry! It's troubling to hear that sort of thing out of nowhere, isn't it? But I—"

"Troubling? I'm not troubled in the slightest. I'm terribly entertained. Really, Aileen is rather adorable. To think she'd be tricked by a woman as pathetic as you."

"Huh…?!"

With a sharp noise, a crack runs through one of the pillars that supports the throne. Ignoring it, Claude walks quietly as the storm of his emotions rages.

"However, the idea that Cedric is the cause of it is unpleasant."

It was Aileen's love for Cedric that had dazzled her to the point where a woman of this caliber could deceive her.

Claude can't help but wonder if Aileen is seeing him out of a faint lingering desire to retaliate against Cedric. Is that why one of her conditions for escorting her is for him to be "better than Master Cedric"?

Why is it? Even as a possibility, it's inexcusable. Even if it's a delusion, he wants to rip it apart.

Has he always been so petty? Or is it because he's a demon?

"I've lost interest in this."

As he speaks, the storm stops dead. Claude puts his face right up to the human girl's nose. His eyes are stone-cold.

"Begone, woman. I'm busy."

"Huh…? B-but I—I came to grant your wish…"

"You cannot grant my wish. I don't even want you to."

The flustered girl's form begins to fade. The fact that she isn't forcibly teleported in the blink of an eye is probably due to the fact that she really does have some sort of resistance to magic.

However, Claude has completely lost interest already. He turns his back on her, facing Beelzebuth.

"Let's go, Beelzebuth. We're late."

"Yes, sire. But outside the forest—"

"Keith will be taking care of it. At any rate, they won't be able to come in."

"U-um— Please wait! Wh-why? What is it? What did I do wrong?"

The girl, who's become as thin as mist, shakes her head in confusion, mussing her hair.

His eyes cold, Claude gives her a simple explanation.

"I don't have the slightest interest in you. That's all."

She's probably never been rejected by anyone in her life. Her shocked expression makes that perfectly clear. An instant later, the noisy human woman is gone.

With a snap of his fingers, he repairs the damaged throne, then straightens his hair and clothes and glances at his pocket watch.

The soiree is well underway.

"Master Cedric. What is the meaning of this? I believe I am an invited guest."

"You brazen little— Lilia has disappeared! It has to be your doing!"

Descending from the raised landing, his footsteps sharp and angry, Cedric comes right up to Aileen, whose arms have been firmly pinioned by the guards. The gentle strains of the orchestra cut off. Everyone is watching them, holding their breath.

"Marcus reported the fact that you're attempting to join forces with the demons. If anything happens to Lilia, there'll be hell to pay!"

"And why would I abduct Lady Lilia?"

"Probably from misplaced resentment, because she 'stole' me away."

Aileen lowers her head, so that she can bite back a smile. It isn't clear how Cedric has interpreted the sight of her biting her lip; his tone softens slightly.

"Even though I held this soiree as an opportunity for you to redeem yourself...! You're always like this. You never hesitate to trample on others' goodwill."

When she surreptitiously glances at the landing, she spots her father. His expression is stern, but it's the face he wears when he's desperately trying not to smirk. How wonderful that he's controlling himself in public.

There are great nobles in attendance as well, as we anticipated. Naturally, the emperor and empress aren't here, but...

She considered the possibility that the same people who'd been at the school party would all be here as well, in an extension of their little game, but apparently, they couldn't manage that at a soiree hosted by the crown prince. However, Cedric doesn't understand what that means.

Those great nobles are here to see how Cedric, who will be graduating from the academy shortly, conducts himself as the crown prince.

"Those threatening letters were your doing as well, weren't they? Tell me! Where is Lilia?"

"I haven't the faintest idea. Perhaps she grew tired of you and left, Master Cedric?"

"It's pointless to try to paint Lilia as a villain and lure me to you that way."

What unwavering optimism. She'd love to emulate that.

"Master Cedric. I haven't plotted Lady Lilia's abduction. In the first place, what proof do you have? Have you conducted a thorough investigation?"

"You're still being evasive... I don't need anything like that. Only an incompetent would use the citizens' tax money to pay for a useless investigation. In any case, who besides you would have a reason for doing a thing like this?!"

"...Really, why did I ever fall for such an incompetent man?"

Her voice rings out more loudly than she expected.

Cedric blinks.

"—What did you just say?"

"I said I wondered why I'd fallen for such a foolish, incompetent, good-for-nothing man with no future potential. Was that clear enough?"

He falls silent. This time, he apparently hasn't misheard her.

"Master Cedric. I shall say it one more time: I have not abducted Lady Lilia."

"...Y-you're still making excuses? You probably thought Lilia would keep you from reconciling with me."

"Reconcile? Even if someone paid me, I would not take you back, Master Cedric."

"—Lies! You told me you still admired me. Obviously, you still pine for me!"

Oh, is that what lies behind this grand delusion? Eyes cold, Aileen spits out her words.

"This is the problem with men."

"Wh-what?"

"I said I 'did admire' you. Past tense. At this point, I don't have the smallest scrap of interest in you. Refrain from such misinterpretations, would you please? I don't love you."

Cedric is stunned, a foolish expression on his face. Sighing, Aileen repeats herself.

"Let me say it again: I do not love you. I have no lingering attachment to you, I want nothing more to do with you, and to be honest, simply breathing the same air as you makes me feel ill. I am eager to end our engagement, and so I've come here today to request that you let me sign that paper."

"...Wh-why?! That can't be. That's not— I—I get it. You're still trying to court my attention, aren't you?!"

"Huh? —Ow!"

He's grabbed her jaw roughly.

Cedric's eyes are intense and glaring, and Aileen can't help but gulp.

"Tell me the truth. It was you who kidnapped Lilia, wasn't it? You weren't able to forget me, and jealousy drove you to this madness."

Fortunately, maybe because Cedric's attitude has stunned the guards who are holding her arms, their grip slackens. She grasps Cedric's wrists with her newly freed hands, attempting to tear his hands away from her. However, they don't budge. It's all she can do just to breathe.

"We don't want to start a needless war, either. If you admit you took Lilia, I'll take your emotional state into consideration. This is my act of mercy. You are the daughter of Duke d'Autriche, and I will respect that position!"

"Wh-who would—?"

"M-Master Cedric. Whatever the circumstances, she is a lady, and you really mustn't—"

"Hold your tongue! I am the crown prince. Don't presume to tell me what to do. This is my woman!"

Who's your *woman?!* Her anger nearly blinds her. In that moment, a cry goes up.

A looming figure emerging from behind her leaves Cedric

paralyzed with fear. Freed at last, Aileen looks back. She sees her own shadow.

Thick front legs, and a maw that seems fully capable of swallowing a human whole. Savage claws and sharp fangs. A demon.

The fenrir's mother! Why—? No, this isn't the time for that!

"You mustn't! Go back! If you hurt any humans—"

The demon opens her huge mouth. At the sight of those fangs, Cedric screams:

"Eee—W-WAAAAUuuuuugh!"

Then the fenrir spits on him.

"......"

In a moment, silence fills the entire hall.

Cedric, who is now sticky from head to toe with spittle, freezes up, petrified.

Snorting, the fenrir quietly settles down beside Aileen. Aileen, who's risen to her feet, looks from the fenrir to Cedric, who's sunk to the floor in a miserable heap, and back again.

—Then she covers her mouth.

"...He may not be much of one, but spitting on a crown prince... Ha-ha, ha-ha-ha! What a comedy."

She puts out a hand and strokes the fenrir's huge furry body. It feels nice to the touch.

"Did you dutifully come to repay me? To think you'd leave the barrier... That goes against Master Claude's orders, you know."

"Rowr."

"...I'm all right. Tell the others so as well, please."

With that, she smacks her lightly.

"Thank you for saving me. Now go, if you would. Leave the rest to me."

The fenrir looks back at Aileen with intelligent eyes. Then the creature gracefully reenters her shadow.

The demon's disappearance seems to break the tension. The assembled guests all look at one another.

Aileen draws a deep breath, then looks down at Cedric, who's still on the ground.

"That would cool a century-long romance in a stroke."

"...Wh...wha...?"

"Where are the documents I need to sign? Up on the landing, perhaps?"

"Wait—wait! I wasn't finished yet!"

Aileen starts to walk away, heels clicking, but Cedric grabs the hem of her dress.

She frowns at his sticky hand, but he's too pathetic to kick off. She gazes at Cedric with pity in her eyes.

"Wh-what's that face for—? What is it?! Why should I be subjected to that look from the likes of you?! You're the one who's losing her engagement!"

"And I'm delighted. Thank you very much."

"Why, *why*?! I'm the only one who would endure a woman like you! Bow your head! Your engagement has been broken by the crown prince, you're ruined, and no one will ever—"

"M-Master Cedric!"

A soldier rushes up, nearly falling over himself. He's so distracted that he doesn't even register Cedric's wretched appearance. The man gasps, his mouth working.

"Uh, I... Prince Claude has... The demon king— In the sky...!"

Right then, the domed glass ceiling shatters.

Screaming, everyone crouches down, covering their heads. Even Aileen quails back reflexively.

However, not a single shard of glass falls. They hang suspended in midair.

Threading between the glittering fragments, two figures descend from above. One is a demon, his pitch-black wings unfurled. However, as he stands behind and a little to the side of his master, he is dressed in a military uniform with decorative gold cords and cannot be mistaken for anything but the epitome of a knight.

The figure who steps forward possesses beauty of a kind that, once seen, is never forgotten. The diabolical king's deep-crimson eyes shine. He snaps his fingers, and the fragments of glass move as one, returning to the ceiling.

In the silent hall, Cedric's hoarse voice echoes.

"Bro...ther... Why are you...here...?"

"Was it you who sent soldiers to the forest?"

The surrounding crowd froze at the demon king's entrance, but hearing that, a stir runs through it. The reactions of the aristocrats on the platform are particularly striking. The chancellor and ministers—Rudolph included—exchange glances, then quickly issue instructions of some sort.

"If you are the crown prince, I ask you refrain from doing something so thoughtless. Do you intend to give me a pretext for destroying the country?"

Cedric's face grows pale.

Apparently, Claude doesn't intend to rebuke him any further. He gazes straight at Aileen.

"I've kept you waiting. My apologies."

"...No. I hadn't waited that long."

"That dress suits you very well."

He smiles at her kindly, without warning, and her cheeks

flush. She blinks, trying to camouflage that heat, but she isn't able to answer him well. On seeing the gesture, Cedric—who's still holding her skirt—stares in abject shock.

"Aileen... Don't tell me you...!"

"Have you finished signing?"

"N-no, not yet."

"Hurry and get it over with. Once it's done, you will officially no longer be Cedric's fiancée. I don't relish the idea of escorting another man's betrothed, much less the fiancée of my younger half brother."

He whispers the words sweetly, as if they're pillow talk, and Aileen averts her face a little to conceal her embarrassment.

"I—I know that. Just a moment."

"Wait... Wait, Aileen. Did you really not kidnap Lilia?"

Aileen looks down at Cedric, who's by her feet.

His expression is uneasy, and it sparks a similar memory. *"Everyone's thinking,* His older brother's the brilliant one, so why...? *They're laughing at me behind my back."* His profile looked lonely then.

Don't get discouraged. You can do this just as well. After all, I'm on your side. She wishes she told him that properly just once.

"...Isaac."

Isaac has been watching the scene play out from a distance, and when she calls his name, he looks just a little reluctant. However, promptly resigning himself, he comes over to her as beckoned.

"You're too soft, Aileen. This could've been your trump card."

"Never mind that. You and the others are my trump cards."

"You're...Count Lombard's..."

Isaac roughly smacks a sheaf of papers onto Aileen's palm, shoots a glance at Cedric, then turns on his heel. As Cedric follows him with his eyes, Aileen holds out the sheaf of papers she's been given.

"These are the threatening letters received by Lady Lilia. I collected the ones that had been thrown on the rubbish heap."

"—Wh-what of them?"

"These are the incriminating letters with my name on them. The stationery is manufactured by the Lombard Company. A stack of sheets is pasted together at the very top, so that each sheet may be turned over individually. There are twenty sheets per set. As part of the design, a pattern is punched through them, and the area around it has been infused with a certain fragrance."

As she speaks, Aileen unfolds the crumpled, threatening letters.

The shape of a rose has been punched through the lower right-hand corner. The area around it is discolored from the perfume. All a part of the distinctive design.

"In this design, the sheets are pasted together, and then the whole stack is punched and perfumed. All the work is done by hand. As a result, if you layer them over each other, like this—sheets from the same set will overlap perfectly. Both the punched pattern, and the perfume stain. Conversely, if the sheets are from different sets, even if they're of the same design, they won't overlap."

Sheets that overlap perfectly, and sheets that don't, although their design is the same. Aileen demonstrates this very clearly to Cedric, then finally takes out the invitation to the soiree, which he sent her.

"When you invited me to this soiree, Lady Lilia very kindly sent me a letter."

As she speaks, she opens the letter. Then she layers it over one of the threatening letters.

The important part is neither the handwriting nor the content. It's the fact that those two sheets of stationery overlap perfectly.

Cedric's eyes go very wide.

"I will keep the letter from Lady Lilia. However, I offer this piece of evidence to you, Master Cedric. Do with it as you will."

"...Wh-what does this mean?"

"Think about it for yourself. After all, in a moment, I will no longer be your fiancée."

Cedric gazes at Aileen, looking as if she's slapped him across the face.

Aileen smiles back somberly.

"Master Cedric— I did admire you."

"......"

"I hope you and Lady Lilia will be happy together. Farewell."

She draws away smoothly, and Cedric drops his hand to the floor.

Without looking back, Aileen makes her way to the flight of stairs. No one stops her.

Up on the landing, two documents have been set out for her. One is for the transfer of the deed to her business. Aileen scans its clauses, checking them over, then quickly signs it.

The other document, which has no particular clauses to check, is the written dissolution of her engagement.

And with this, it's over.

She writes her own name beside Cedric's, then sets down the quill pen.

Now Aileen Lauren d'Autriche is free.

She sweeps a graceful curtsy to the assembled great nobles, who have been watching her closely from the side of the landing. Then, as she sets a hand on the banister of the stairs, preparing to descend from the platform, Claude extends a hand to her from below.

"Lady Aileen Lauren d'Autriche. Now that you are your own woman, please grant me the right to your first dance."

Asking for a lady's first dance is a conventional courtship tactic. However, the same sort of innocent shyness she felt when she only just made her society debut wells up within her.

Giving a small nod, she places her hand in his. Cedric is behind Claude, and she can't see him now.

That's why she doesn't notice.

"...Ha-ha...ha-ha, ha... You *did* admire me? You, with my brother?"

She doesn't register the sound of the letter being crumpled in his fist, either.

"Don't think you'll get away with betraying me...!"

Or his dark smile. Or the obsession in his glazed eyes.

A slightly rotund moon hangs in the sky. It's a clear night, and there are no clouds. No doubt the view from the flying carriage would have been a good one.

However, being escorted home to her mansion properly in a carriage that travels over the ground shows that he is conforming to social norms for her sake, and this carries a quiet thrill of its own.

"Really, thank you so much for today."

Having descended from the carriage Denis built, Aileen

extends her heartfelt thanks to Claude, who's standing before the mansion's front entrance.

"As promised, you were a perfect escort."

"You're sure it was all right to leave after a single dance?"

"Yes. No doubt word of the Oberon Trading Firm reached my father's ears. If we induce the d'Autriche duchy to act as an intermediary for the company, it will result in more than enough profit."

The d'Autriche duchy already has information on the Oberon Trading Firm, which no one was familiar with but everyone was talking about. That foresight would prove to be more of an advantage to the d'Autriches than the money the company itself would generate.

"Because you were with me, Master Claude, no one who saw the dissolution of my engagement to Master Cedric will have assumed that I've been miserably cast aside, and the suspicion over the kidnapping incident should go away as well. Besides, they found Lady Lilia in the end…"

When she's gotten that far, Aileen glances up at Claude.

"…It was you, wasn't it, Master Claude?"

"What was me?"

"The one who dropped Lady Lilia into the cesspool."

"I have no idea what you're talking about."

Claude feigns ignorance, looking innocent, and she feels rather appalled.

Just after she'd danced that first dance with Claude, a report that the missing Lilia had been found in the imperial castle's cesspool was spreading. The location being what it is, the idea that Aileen had plotted to have her kidnapped by demons promptly dissolved. Everyone who heard the news went stiff, and all they'd been able to do was feel sorry for the poor girl who'd wound up somewhere unspeakable.

No sooner had Cedric heard the report than he dashed out, along with Marcus, who'd returned from the demon king's forest. The host of the soiree, Cedric himself, had left in the middle, and although Rudolph and the other great nobles casually smoothed the matter over and kept up appearances, that response was unwise of him.

...Opinions of Master Cedric and Lady Lilia have fallen. There's the fact that they couldn't even host a soiree properly, and on top of that, the rashness of nearly starting a battle with the demons...

It will probably be overlooked as youthful recklessness, but Aileen feels uneasy about the future.

Something resembling the kidnapping incident had occurred, but the announcement of Cedric and Lilia's engagement was canceled, and so from this point on, she isn't sure how the events from the game will progress. Considered optimistically, she may have broken free from the Cedric route, but she can't afford to be careless. For example...

"...Lady Lilia was charming, wasn't she?"

Once she's murmured the words, she regrets them. However, she can't stop.

"Sh-she's popular, you know; they say her smile soothes the heart. She isn't a striking beauty like me, but her skin has this luster, her hair is silky, and if she wears a gown and does her makeup properly, she's so lovely that you'd hardly recognize her. The first time I saw her in formal wear, even I was startled."

"...Really?"

"She's far better at cooking and sewing than I am, too. It wasn't as if Lady Lilia was on my mind, but I only learned those things in the past year, in a rushed way. Besides, the way she speaks is gentle, and more than anything, she's honest and genuine, and she respects her companions, and she doesn't work them hard..."

"Aileen."

She doesn't think the Claude route can have been unlocked. However, that girl is the heroine. If they talked as they had in the game and a flag has been tripped, she can't completely deny the fact that it might be enough to make Claude a repeat of Cedric.

"Men appreciate women like her, don't they? I'm— Ouch! Ow, ow, ow, ow, ow!"

"These stretch surprisingly well."

"What are you doing?!"

He reaches his hands to tug on her cheeks again, and she evades them. Claude shrugs.

"You don't have to worry: You are lovable, and she isn't my type."

She gapes at him. Then she blushes; it dawns on her what she was really nervous about.

Suddenly feeling awkward, her voice tapers off, as if she's sulking.

"...I-I'm sure you talked with Lady Lilia. What an odd thing to say after that."

"Do you think so? All she said was something about making my wish come true."

"Your wish, Master Claude? Now there's a difficult task..."

"What, you know my wish?"

"You don't want to give up either the demons or the humans."

The answer comes out quite naturally.

"After all, you looked happy when you watched the demons and Denis's team work together."

Even though he was the one who posed the question, Claude looks surprised. As she thinks, *He tends to stifle his emotions, but I'm starting to be able to read his expression*, he abruptly breaks into a broad smile.

"...I also wish to make you cry, you know."

"I reject that wish!"

She responds instantly, and Claude gives a soft laugh. She's so startled hearing him laugh for once that she gulps.

"Too bad— That's enough for today; go and rest. I'm sure you're tired."

"Y-yes. I shall... Hmm? What?"

He's pulled her closer, and Aileen blinks. Stopping just beyond her eyelashes, Claude checks with her.

"I was a perfect escort, correct?"

A good-bye kiss. She isn't boorish enough to ask, *Why here?* You could call it etiquette, technically.

However, there's a smoldering passion in Claude's red eyes. As if his gaze has scorched them, Aileen's cheeks flush, and she closes her own eyes, her heart racing.

This isn't like her. Growing so nervous just waiting for a single, formulaic kiss...

Soft and featherlight, Claude's lips brush her cheek. As if she's been burned, heat runs in waves from that spot across her whole body— and behind her eyelids, a silent scream sears itself into her mind.

"Fall. Meet your doom. There isn't a single human I want to protect anymore—!!"

Aileen's eyes open wide. She sees a gibbous moon that's just one day from reaching its zenith.

Gently drawing back, Claude whispers:

"Good night, Aileen. Pleasant dreams."

"G-good night…"

She's probably managed to make her strained smile seem like an attempt to conceal her embarrassment. First, the carriage disappears from view. Then Claude launches himself off the brick paving, rising into the air with the moon at his back before vanishing into the darkness.

Pressing her hands to her cheeks, feeling as if she might sink to the ground, she leans against a pillar for support.

"I've said it before, but my memories always choose the worst times to return…!"

Thanks to that, she hadn't been able to lose herself in the thrill of the moment. It's absolutely unforgivable.

Not only that, but this time, there also isn't even a week left for her to take action.

"But yes… That's how it was. That's what will turn you into a demon."

She's remembered. She knows why he lost all faith in humans.

He's going to be betrayed. Sold out by the one human he's trusted since childhood.

"You are human. You don't have to come with me."

That was what his black-haired, red-eyed master, a fellow known as the demon king, told him when he left the imperial castle.

How cruel. What else could be expected from a demon king? *I've become an outcast for allying myself with demons, apparently. At this point, I can't even go home, and he still said that without a hint of sarcasm*, he thought. He shook his head and left the castle with him.

Life with the demons hadn't been bad. They were so thoughtless that it gave him headaches sometimes, but that was true of humans as well.

Besides, you're still human yourself. You just might obtain human happiness someday.

So please... I'll make your wish come true for you. Just don't give up on humans.

"You need land? Sell it to the demon lord? Yes, that can be arranged."

Still, he thought it. He, who could only be human, went and had that thought.

"In exchange, give us demons that are worth something. The demon king trusts you deeply; no doubt you'll find a clever way to cull the herd. If you can't do it, we won't give you any land. The demons can just cannibalize one another in those cramped quarters you call home. When all's said and done, the demon king won't wage war against humans."

It was only supposed to be one time. He'd only have to dirty his hands once. That was what he thought.

He was still a child then. He didn't know that once your hands were stained, it was impossible to become clean.

"Did we sign a contract saying we'd sell at this price? Come now, it's fine. Just sell us more demons."

"You don't want us to take that land away, do you? Otherwise, the demons will lose their home again."

"We tricked you? What a preposterous accusation. You're the one who's betraying the demon king."

In a world like this, you just might be happier as a demon.

The thought was always on his mind. It was very human of him.

"Oh, are you awake, Master Keith?"

Opening his sleep-dazed eyes, Keith realizes that someone's sitting on his bed, looking down at him. The morning sun lances through the gap in the curtains behind her, and he can't make out her face clearly. However, he recognizes that elegant, bell-like voice, and the golden hair that looks almost misty in the sunlight.

The problem, of course, is that this is his room, so why is she here?

"...Miss Aileen. Stealing into a man's bedchamber, and not even under the cover of night—"

As he tries to sit up, a blade gleams near his throat. When he glances over quickly, moving only his eyes, Beelzebuth is crouched low beside the bed, lurking.

"Beelzebuth. This is the fifth layer. What are you doing outside the barrier?"

"Right now, I am Aileen's faithful hound."

"That's lower than a knight, you know. You're all right with that?"

"She told me it was for Master Claude's sake."

That answer makes him laugh at himself inwardly.

Did she stumble onto the truth after making a connection with the embezzlement? Well, there was no way the fact that I was meekly over-looking it wouldn't make her suspicious.

Not only that, but she's also stolen a march on him. How very clever. Her instincts are good, too, and she's got spine. There's no telling how she coaxed Beelzebuth into this, but she's clearly won his confidence as well.

However, what has she learned about, and how much, and to what extent? She can't have found much concrete proof.

"Master Keith? You're doing something bad, aren't you? Unbeknownst to Master Claude."

Still wearing his usual smile, Keith says nothing. The girl, who's as human as he is, allows her lips to curve into a smile.

"Would you let me join you?"

"Huh?"

The unexpected proposal makes him frown. In that moment, with a rustle, she dangles a document in front of his nose.

His eyes go wide with shock. Forgetting about the blade at his throat, he tries to leap up, but she whisks the paper out of reach.

"H-h-h-how in the world did you get that?!"

"Heh-heh-heh. Master Keith. Your one weakness is that you have no human allies— Let me tell you something useful. You're clever, so no doubt you'll understand. Before long, the Maid of the Sacred Sword will awaken. It's Lady Lilia."

How could she possibly know a thing like that? Even as that

question rises in his mind, so does the events that would naturally follow such a development.

"...If she has the sacred sword, even the demon king will be no match for her. She's bound to make an attempt on Master Claude's life. But the sacred sword only works on demons; it won't affect him while he's human. Will she set some sort of trap to change him into a demon? —Ah, that's what you told Beelzebuth to enlist his help, isn't it?"

"Correct. I'd expect no less of you, Master Keith. I do believe you know more about what goes on in the world than anyone else in the abandoned castle."

"Well, I am a high-ranking official in the court... However, this all only holds true if the Maid of the Sacred Sword actually awakens, you know."

"You'll just have to trust me there. Based on that information, then, we have a pressing problem: According to legend, when the demon king—Master Claude—becomes unable to contain his anger, hatred, or other negative emotion toward humans, he'll assume his demon form, transforming into a dragon, and truly become the demon king. That being the case, what scheme do you suppose the humans will attempt?"

"...Sell demons or something, perhaps? If they make the demons suffer, he'll hate humans."

Intentionally, he asks her a leading question. Aileen's eyes go round, and then she laughs a little.

"That's why even though you're this clever, you were taken advantage of, exploited, and died in the game."

"Huh? Game?"

"I'm only talking to myself; pay it no mind. Your answer is half-correct and half-mistaken. The right answer is they'll expose

your betrayal and force him to kill you. If that scheme succeeds, no doubt Master Claude will lose faith in humanity. After
all, he'll have been betrayed by the only human he truly believed
in, and on top of that, he'll have killed that human by his own
hand. What follows that is only natural."

When she points this out to him, Keith's eyes widen. She's
right; as a rule, the demons are inside the barrier, protected. He
himself is much easier to target—and to use.

"As I said earlier: Your one weakness is that you have no
human allies."

Rising from the bed, Aileen Lauren d'Autriche turns around.

"So I have a proposal—make me your ally, won't you?"

She smiles at the traitor.

"We'll need money."

The conference room at the abandoned castle has finally been
finished. In it, Aileen stands tall with her hands on her hips. The
usual members sit to the left and right of her at the round table,
and each responds to her declaration in their own way.

Isaac, who's resting his chin on his hand, looks dubious.

"Money? We cleared Duke d'Autriche's requirement, didn't
we? People are already saying things like 'To think they're
acquainted with the rumored Oberon Trading Firm! We'd expect
nothing less from the d'Autriche duchy's information network.
What's more, their daughter is personally acquainted with the
demon king.' They're really starting to respect you."

"Do you mean we'll be starting a new business? I'm done with the design for the vanity bag we're giving away as a first-time limited-edition bonus to customers who buy a full set of our products."

As Denis speaks, he passes the design around the table. Luc glances at it, then raises his hand.

"I've finished the improvements on that herb vinegar. We'll be able to market it as an agricultural chemical that effectively exterminates harmful insects on crops."

"...But we're short on materials for all of them. At this point in time, mass production isn't possible."

Quartz speaks with his arms crossed and his eyes downcast; he doesn't even look at the design. Aileen turns to the one person who's leaning against the wall instead of sitting at the table.

"Jasper."

"...Yeah, yeah. You're sure?"

"Yes, it's fine. There's no time."

Jasper hands some documents to Aileen. Aileen slides these and enough handwritten plans for everyone across the table.

"The documents are copies. When you've each looked the plans over, dispose of them by tossing them into the fireplace."

"...Huh?!"

Denis, who's nearly cried out, hastily covers his mouth. Luc's eyes go round, and then he puts a hand to his mouth, furiously paging through the document. Scowling, Quartz slowly and carefully reads through the plan Aileen has written.

Isaac, who's the first to finish parsing the document, turns stern eyes on Aileen.

"You're seriously doing this? It's just barely avoids violating the nonaggression pact outright. One wrong step, and we'll suffer massive damages."

"Protecting the demons will benefit the Oberon Trading Firm. Besides, we have a trump card."

"A trump card?"

"Right here—Keith the trump card speaking! She's got me over a barrel, so I'm here to help you out!"

A desperately cheerful voice rings out, and the door of the conference room opens.

Isaac and the others look taken aback. Watching them out of the corner of his eye, Keith crosses the room to stand next to Aileen.

"And just what do you mean by that? I compensated you properly, didn't I?"

"Wow, just listen to you. This is why I loathe people in power! All right, Miss Aileen's lackeys, listen up as I leak information."

"Lackeys..."

"Don't worry; starting today, I'm a fellow lackey! When Miss Aileen said, 'Would you lend me Master Keith?' and begged him prettily, the demon king said okay, and boy, had he better watch his back because I'll remember this! On his own, he doesn't even know where we keep the tea! Beelzebuth can't make tea, all right?!"

"Is this guy okay in the head?" Isaac asks, jerking a thumb in his direction.

Aileen nods.

"He may be even better at scheming than you. After all, what he did to Master Claude was—"

"Yes, okay, let's not talk about that sort of thing inside the barrier, hmm? That stubborn demon king is absolutely listening! So how are you going to save my humble self, Your Majesty, Queen Aileen?"

His desperate cheer subsiding instantly, Keith sets a hand against his chest, speaking in an exaggerated way.

Aileen beams at him.

"I'm merely redeeming you from a false charge."

"A false charge, hmm? Well, yes, all right. I am the demon king's left-hand man, after all. I'll guzzle down the pure and the corrupt together as is required of me."

Exhaling dramatically, Keith pushes up the rim of his spectacles.

Aileen looks around the group.

"You will do it, won't you? I trust you all. And I need your strength."

Everyone glances up, then sighs.

Taking reactions as acceptance, Aileen sets her hands on the table.

"If there are flaws in the plan, Isaac, you correct them. Jasper, I want you and Master Keith to gather solid proof and information. New information should be shared as you find it. Denis, Luc, and Quartz, you start work on your end immediately."

On Aileen's instructions, Isaac is the first to toss his plan into the blazing fireplace. Then Denis and Luc—and finally, Quartz, when he's finished reading the materials—burn both the documents and the plan.

"We don't even have a week. As usual, get to work quickly."

"Aileen! Enemy attack! Enemy attack! They're back!"

Almond bursts out of her shadow, and Aileen turns around. Isaac and the others, who've all been gazing at the fireplace, scowl.

"Enemy attack? The business about the kidnapping the other day was already settled, wasn't it?"

"**No! Master Claude's angry!**"

"—Lady Lilia and the others are here, aren't they?"

As the rest look startled, Almond shrieks, "**Bingo!**"

Aileen gives a dauntless smile. In the fireplace behind her, the letters *Demon Trafficking* burn up and vanish.

Keith Eigrid. The second son of the venerable Viscount Eigrid, he's two years older than Claude, and even before Claude was born, it had been decided that he would serve as the prince's attendant and playmate.

The people around them begun to suspect that Claude might be the demon king when he was five years old. It started when Keith nearly drowned in a garden pond, and Claude saved him using magic. When Cedric was born and the struggle over the succession began, there were several attempts on Claude's life, and at that point, it was discovered that demons would come to his rescue without fail.

The emperor and the others were hiding Master Claude... Although, I'm not sure whether it was out of love or concern for what the world would think.

Once he'd saved Keith's life, they could no longer completely hide the fact that he was the demon king. Keith must have blamed himself for it. That's why he's continued to serve him loyally to this day.

...Even if it means going against the demon king's wishes. It's a supremely human way of doing things.

Aileen should have guessed when she heard about that land

Claude had bought for the demons' sake. After all, there's no way he could have managed to buy a count's entire domain for cheap. Young Keith had raised the capital to make that purchase by selling demons. He'd probably offered some of the demons who'd come seeking refuge. If it happened before they crossed the barrier, Claude wouldn't have noticed.

However, what should have been a single transaction ended up occurring again and again.

If he refused at any point, the land would be repossessed. He'd been neatly trapped, and there was no one he could turn to for help. He'd kept on fighting all alone. He'd taken on the unbearably heavy choice of sacrificing a handful of demons in order to save the rest of them.

The transactions continued because they were profitable for the humans involved as well. Lilia's awakening as the Maid of the Sacred Sword would make that whole arrangement come apart at the seams.

...After that, it's just as Master Keith guessed. Once the demon king is gone, humans won't fear the demons anymore.

If there was no demon king, the demons wouldn't flock together. Their intelligence would fall, and most of them would degenerate into vermin who were merely minor nuisances. If humans used their tools and knowledge and fought in small groups, it wouldn't be very hard to hunt the demons down. Not only that, but some of their parts could also be sold for incredibly high prices. Humans would become the hunters.

In that case, it is inevitable that a faction would be created that preferred to eliminate the demon king rather than rely on the nonaggression pact. After all, one stroke with the sacred sword, and the demon king would vanish forever.

However, the sacred sword is a weapon for fighting demons

and is said not to work on humans. While Claude is still human, they can't kill him with it.

In which case, he simply has to be turned into a true demon... This was the progression that triggered the "demon king's awakening" event.

In the game, Keith screamed that he'd done it because he wanted money. He sneered as he told Claude that he'd only served him because it had let him do good business. He cursed the demon king, saying he should just die.

However, that had probably been a kindhearted lie.

"You see, I keep thinking... If Master Claude turned into a demon, he might be happier."

That's what Keith said this morning, when he gave in to Aileen's proposal. By rights, the choice he'd made should have been Claude's decision. In the game, he'd probably thought that if the alternative was making Claude bear that guilt and stay a human who still felt sympathy for Keith, then he wanted him to hate all humans—Keith included—and become a demon.

The game proceeded just like that, starting with Claude flying into a rage, killing Keith with his own hands, losing all faith in humans, and finally transforming into a dragon and shedding his last vestiges of humanity.

It was common during the Cedric route for the emperor to give Cedric the task of resolving the illegal trafficking of demons before graduation. Lilia helped him, suspected Keith, and tipped off Claude. Accompanying Cedric's party, she tried to raid a transaction site and arrest Keith, but instead, they ran into Claude, who had killed Keith. Then, after Claude despaired and turned into a dragon, she told him *"I'll put an end to your sorrow"* and used the sacred sword to destroy him.

Parenthetically, during the Claude route, which appeared on the second playthrough, the story shifted to one where she managed to keep him human. When Claude had been hurt by Keith's betrayal, she soothed him, telling him, *"I'm here,"* and restored his humanity. Then, having decided to spend his life with Lilia, the Maid of the Sacred Sword, Claude decided to abdicate his position as demon king to avoid standing in opposition to her. He sealed all the demons into the spirit world, then lived as an ordinary human.

Now that she's regained all her memories of those events, Aileen has just one thing to say:

"What a perfectly useless heroine...!!"

The moment game Lilia realized Keith was suspicious, she should have considered what would happen to Claude, then acted accordingly. All Lilia did in the game was force Claude to see Keith's betrayal, hurt him, then either have the gall to say *"I'll put an end to your sorrow"* and destroy him or tell him *"I'm here"* and make him leave everything behind. How completely irresponsible. Aileen thoroughly disapproves.

Not only that, but as it turns out, the answer to the question of how Lilia—the Maid of the Sacred Sword, who's incompatible with demons—and Claude—who wants to protect the demons—managed to be together is that Claude abandoned the demons, a development that strikes Aileen as completely beyond belief.

I refuse to allow Master Claude to choose a future like that.

If it's up to her, Aileen will get Claude everything he wants.

She won't let him cast aside the demons. She won't let him kill his precious attendant.

Everything she needs in order to make that happen will be determined by the foundations she lays. Such is the nature of battles.

"—I'm telling you to leave."

At the sound of Claude's low voice, the door to the parlor swings open on its own, and a blizzard blusters all the way out into the corridor.

Apparently, the "anonymous report" event is already underway.

Beelzebuth and the others are in the corridor, holding their breath as they watch the scene play out.

The whole group looks at her uneasily. Aileen smiles, nodding.

"But, Master Claude, it's true. Keith is selling demons. We came to tell you because we thought if you weren't already aware, you'd be hurt..."

Lilia, who's sitting on the sofa in the parlor, hangs her head. Beside her, Cedric instantly speaks up, sounding critical.

"It's just as Lilia says, Brother. We could have ignored you and moved forward with the investigation on our own, but Lilia said that would be too awful. That's why we've come to talk to you in secret."

"Don't tell me the demons were sold on your orders. Were you planning to pick a fight with the humans by claiming we're in violation of the nonaggression pact?"

Marcus's provocation makes Claude glare with his red eyes. The furniture rattles, and the floor and the ground tremble. It's an earthquake.

"Enough of—"

"Getting angry is useless. Lilia's the reincarnation of the Maid of the Sacred Sword."

At Marcus's boast, the shaking stops. Lilia bows her head, seeming embarrassed.

"W-we don't know that for sure yet... I keep asking you not to spread that rumor."

"What are you talking about? There's no mistake. Even the church acknowledged it. More than anything, the sword that materializes from your body— If that's not the sacred sword, then what is it? It has that demon-eradicating radiance!"

"That's right, Lilia. You should have confidence in yourself. That's why Father left the resolution of the illegal demon trafficking to us."

Apparently, Lilia's power as the Maid of the Sacred Sword has already awakened. As a result, Cedric and Marcus have grown even more infatuated with her. They don't seem to have registered the fact that they've misspoken.

"In this country, the blood of the Maid of the Sacred Sword runs thickest in Aileen. However, she was a far cry from the Maid. I was right to choose you—"

"This is quite an intriguing conversation. 'Demon-eradicating,' you say?"

Aileen enters the room, heels clicking on the floor. Chill air flows past her feet.

"That's the first I've heard of it. Even though killing demons is forbidden by the nonaggression pact?"

"...Aileen."

Claude looks up, and Aileen sits down beside him. She smiles.

"Both your heads and your tongues are as light as ever, I see. I believe eradicating demons is the story you should refrain from spreading around, not the one about the Maid of the Sacred Sword. Since it is a violation of the nonaggression pact, you understand."

"Th-the demons only saw the sacred sword and took to their heels! Lilia didn't even scratch them!"

"Well, that's marvelous news. Isn't it, Master Claude?"

She drops a hand onto Claude's clenched fist. At that, finally, the cold air stops swirling around her feet.

"What was it you were talking about, then? Something about Master Keith illicitly selling demons?"

"Th-that's right."

"Gracious, that's ridiculous. Away with you, I insist."

"R-ridiculous?! That's so mean! Don't you feel sorry for the demons?!"

"But selling demons isn't a crime by any definition, you know."

Aileen tilts her head. Lilia widens her eyes.

Even Cedric and Marcus are staring, stunned. She can't deal with all of them.

"What *is* forbidden is harming demons. Trafficking demons is not. People have merely decided not to do it because it would anger Master Claude. It's a matter of ethics. In the first place, even if Master Keith has been illicitly selling demons, exactly what crime would humans arrest him for?"

"I—I wish to avoid conflict between demons and humans! If we don't, since I am the Maid of the Sacred Sword, I'll end up having to kill Master Claude, you know..."

"Master Claude is still human. You wouldn't be able to kill him with the sacred sword even if you wanted to. To summarize..."

Without giving Lilia time to get depressed and be fussed over, Aileen smiles elegantly.

"...you aren't needed here, so off with you now, there's a dear. Wouldn't it be better to spend your time diligently studying in preparation for becoming the empress? I haven't been hearing very good rumors about you."

"How cruel...!"

Springing to her feet, Lilia runs out, crying. Hastily, Cedric and Marcus chase after her. Exhaling so deeply that her shoulders droop, Aileen summons Almond.

"Master Claude's power may not be enough. Watch those three from the sky until they've left the forest properly, please. Mind you, you mustn't get too close; the power of the Maid of the Sacred Sword is real."

"Understood!"

Almond, who's been perched on top of Beelzebuth's head, flaps away. Claude starts to speak.

"Don't do anything dange— Very well. I'll leave it to your judgment."

"Good. Right now, more than the demons, you need to protect Master Keith. Do you understand?"

The Maid of the Sacred Sword has appeared. In order to capitalize on Claude's vulnerability, the people who've been after him will think to strike at Keith, the easiest target. Because he's human.

"...Is there something substantial enough to make them suspect him?"

Claude, who's spoken in a murmur, may have picked up on something. When she glances over, Keith is there in the corridor.

Aileen signals him with her eyes. He looks up at the ceiling for a moment, then walks briskly over to Claude.

Then he kneels, bowing his head.

"Master Claude. There's something I must tell you."

"...Out with it."

"Hoooowever, the thing is, it's going to have to wait until I finish the job Miss Aileen has assigned to me."

He glances at her casually, and Aileen looks blank.

"Once this incident is cleared away, confess everything to Master Claude of your own accord. Don't make arbitrary choices; ask your master for his decision. Not doing so was your very first mistake."

Aileen's the one who told him that. Since that's so, he could just as well confess now.

"I mustn't leave my mistake standing and end up sabotaging you. I am your left-hand man, after all."

With that, Keith turns to face Claude. The loyalty in his gaze is clear and sincere.

Claude must have sensed this as well. Resting his chin in his hand, he sighs.

"...All right. When the time comes, be prepared. Depending on the situation, I may have to punish you."

"Understood, my king."

"Also, I know where the tea is. I just don't know how to make it."

"I do beg your pardon, sire."

Aileen, who's been listening to this exchange from beside them, quietly begins to rise to her feet, but for some reason, Claude pulls her down to sit on his lap.

"Wh-what is it? And here I was going to leave you to yourselves."

"Where's the fun in being left alone with another man? You're rather odd about that sort of thing. And what's this? You're using Keith as you please, you've won Beelzebuth over, and you're keeping something from me. What are you plotting?"

From behind, Claude slowly strokes her throat with the tip of his finger. Scowling fiercely, she slams an elbow into his solar plexus. He must have had his guard down; he takes the full brunt of the blow and groans.

"I am particularly good at fending off perverts."

"Perverts...?"

For the first time in quite a while, lightning strikes outside. Apparently, that shocked him. Then she hears rain begin to fall; that can't possibly have made him sad, right?

Keith bursts out laughing, while Beelzebuth and the others look flustered. Crossing in front of them, Aileen leaves the parlor quickly, so that they won't catch a glimpse of her prim face and reddened cheeks. When Claude does things like that and she overreacts, she's learned that she tends to get dragged into his pace far too easily.

"The demon king's pretty naive, too. One more push was all it would've taken back there."

Isaac, who's waiting in the corridor, is smirking and looking like he knows everything, so while she's at it, she hits him in the solar plexus as well.

From the looks of Claude and Keith, she gets the feeling they've already managed to evade the crucial trigger of the demon king's awakening, which is Claude's despair. However, they've gone too far to turn back, and besides, since Lilia has been discovered to be the Maid of the Sacred Sword, the day when their opponents attempt to exploit that weakness is bound to come.

In that case, she decides it would be best to hurry and simply eliminate all the factors that worry her.

"He should be arriving any minute now. He always hires some toughs, just in case the demons start to fight, so stay near Beelzebuth, Miss Aileen. After all, if anything happens to you, Master Claude will undoubtedly fall into the depths of despair!"

"You're more of a concern than I am, Master Keith. Don't get struck by a stray arrow and die while you're out on the front line."

"Ah, you really don't get it, do you? Master Isaac and the others must have it rough..."

He says the words as if he feels them keenly, and then she's shooed away to the roof of the academy with Beelzebuth, where she'll be able to have a commanding view of the site.

It's late at night. A bright full moon is in the sky. And once again, Aileen finds herself back at the academy—a place she thought she'd probably seen for the last time—behind the dormitory near the Holy Knights' training grounds. The game designers must have wanted to reuse the event's background image.

Of course, by this point, the only remaining major event to be held at the academy is the graduation ceremony, so no students are there. That makes it a convenient location; they wouldn't be spotted, and if a demon did start to rampage, they could let the knights handle it.

"...Hey, girl. Will Keith be all right?"

"What do you mean, 'all right'? Is something worrying you?"

"He...sold demons, didn't he...?"

Beelzebuth was told not to say anything uncalled for, under any circumstances, because it would hurt Claude. As a result, he's been very quiet lately, and even as he speaks now, he's gazing down at the roof.

"I explained why he'd done it right at the start."

"I know that much! I know, but if he wanted land, I would have stolen it for him!"

"If you'd done that, no doubt there would have been a fight."

"And what if there had?! We wouldn't lose to puny humans!"

"I am also a human."

Beelzebuth's head comes up as if he's been stung, and then he looks down again. He may be more wounded than Claude. Because they are demons, the mere betrayal of a companion hurts and saddens them quite severely.

"Master Keith is human as well... And Master Claude—he may be the demon king, but he's still human."

"...I don't understand. Why?"

"You don't have to understand. You don't have to forgive him, either... I doubt Master Keith expects anyone to do that."

Looking down from the roof of the school building, she can see Keith standing all alone in front of the demon cage Denis built. What must he be feeling right now?

"...Master Keith said that when he chose the demons to sell, he was honest to the point of foolishness and explained the situation to them every time."

"What?"

"When he did, the demons who could speak the human language always answered, 'If it will help the demon king and the others, I'll go.' Even the demons who didn't speak went with Master Keith without resisting in the slightest."

"Every time it happened, I was forced to realize that I was merely human."

As he told her that, Keith laughed weakly.

"That's...probably true. I would have said that as well..."

"I imagine you would. And that's why we're taking them back."

"...Huh?"

Beelzebuth blinks at her.

"Apparently, all the transactions have been done by the same person. Every time, he brings an account book with a record of which demons he purchased and how much they cost. He must have information about where the sold demons ended up in that ledger of his as well."

Those records would double as proof that he was involved in trafficking demons.

Regardless of what she said to Lilia and the others, although selling demons isn't a crime, it is an extremely delicate issue. It would also incur the displeasure of the emperor, who had formed the nonaggression pact with the demon king, for causing unnecessary trouble.

Since that was so, if they could just get their hands on that proof, the client wouldn't be able to meddle with Keith any longer.

"Of course, some of the demons have probably been killed. However, as long as they are alive, there is a possibility that we can buy them back. Master Keith is no fool. After he sold them, he put pressure on the places he was able to pressure, so we may find them through those channels as well. Although, it appears that as a result, he couldn't make any forceful moves when his salary and your estate's budget were embezzled."

However, by having Jasper barge in as a third party, while they hadn't been able to get the actual embezzler arrested, they managed to reclaim the lost money.

"True, it's bound to be tiresome, but Master Keith did determine where that fatal edge was. He really is an outstanding attendant. I'd like him for myself. I'd expect no less of the demon king's left-hand man. Isn't that correct, Sir Right Hand?"

When she smiles at him, Beelzebuth responds sulkily.

"That's, well... You're not wrong, but..."

"Besides, in order to buy back as many of the trafficked

demons as we can, and to protect the new demons who are sure to come later, we need Master Keith. Don't we?"

"—I don't like this!" Beelzebuth barks. He sits down heavily on the roof and begins to mutter, "Can't we resolve this by hitting these traffickers? Why? We should just burn them!"

"If we did that, demons who live elsewhere would be attacked. The official stance that the demon king is controlling the demons so that they won't attack humans has created an environment where it's difficult to lay a hand on the demons."

"We should just incinerate them, too! A human town would go up in an instant!"

"Then what if Denis's house were there, for example?"

Possibly because of his interpreting work he's been doing, Beelzebuth has become quite close to Denis. The sword that hangs at his waist was designed by Denis, then ordered through his connections. Maybe because that's so, he answers without hesitating.

"I wouldn't burn it. I have enough control for that."

"Then what if a friend of Denis's with whom you weren't acquainted were there?"

"......"

He falls silent, a sour look on his face. With a troubled smile, Aileen extends a hand toward Beelzebuth's head. Then, as gently as possible, she pats it.

"...What are you playing at?"

"You seem to be giving it some good, hard thought, and I think that's splendid of you. Keep that up and learn all sorts of different things. I'm sure they'll be useful to Master Claude and Master Keith. The truth is, you feel wretched at having made Master Keith fight all alone, and you can't abide that. Isn't that right?"

Beelzebuth grunts, at a loss for words. Aileen keeps stroking his head. *There's a good boy.*

"How long are you going to continue petting me?"

"Until you've cheered up."

"Enough, then! —They're here."

Beelzebuth's sight and hearing are very good, and when he signals her with a glance, she hastily refocuses her gaze on the ground. From a distance, a clearly suspicious group is approaching Keith.

The location and everything else match her memories of the event. It's started.

...Oh? But Lady Lilia and the others aren't in the bushes...

In the game, Lilia's group hid in the shrubbery near the site and watched. However, there's no sign of them. As she's wondering about that, Keith has begun talking with his client.

They're discussing the sale of his companions, and Beelzebuth's expression sours again.

"You mustn't, Master Beelzebuth. Trust Master Keith."

"I know. My role is to stay here and guard you. Both Keith and Denis asked me to. So did the others—and the king, who can't be here himself."

She looks blank. Beelzebuth murmurs:

"If anything happens to you, I'm sure the king won't forgive the humans."

"By the way, may I ask, Count Penne?"

Keith's voice echoes intentionally loud, and it pulls her attention back to the present.

"I hear you've sold the territory I want to Duke d'Autriche."

"...Wh-what are you...talking about?"

A man's unsteady voice feigns ignorance. Keith doesn't waver.

After all, the day Aileen had pressured him to make her his ally, she showed him a sales contract for the land he'd wanted badly enough to sell his companions for.

"Even if you wait and fidget like that, the knights aren't here to collar me yet. The bridge has collapsed, and they're currently taking the long way around."

"Wh-what's the meaning of this?"

"I did think you were at least conscious of the fact that as partners in illegal trafficking, we were in the same boat. To think you were planning to end it by pinning all our crimes on me."

Keith removes his glasses.

When Aileen prompts Beelzebuth with a glance, he lobs a fireball into the sky.

"It really is a shame… And so allow me to take that book—and my leave."

The flames, which shine like a sun in the night sky, are a signal.

As the other man recoils from the sudden light, Keith instantly closes the distance between them, snatches the sales ledger, then knocks him out with the hilt of his sword. At the same time, the demons all burst out of the cage, which had been left unlocked. As Almond wheels overhead, giving directions, they obey, fleeing via the routes that Isaac drilled into them.

"Hey, the demons—"

"Never mind them, get that book back! If that falls into their hands…"

Demons must not attack humans. That is a fundamental principle.

"But if they happen to dig holes or drop potions while they're just playing around, well, that's probably fine, right?"

Isaac laughed when he said it. What is, according to Almond, the vaunted air force of the demon king's army scatters various articles Luc has prepared, including a potion that stings the eyes, and a powder that will make certain people sneeze and their noses run uncontrollably. The humans fall into holes that were dug in advance and stomp through snares that send logs toppling down.

None of these are things the demons could prepare on their own, but this is cutting it very close to violating the nonaggression pact.

Isaac laughed. *"It's not like anybody's gonna die."* She'll have to tell him to restrain himself a bit next time.

"Still, Master Keith certainly is formidable, isn't he...?"

The demons sent to provide backup have withdrawn, and the majority of the sellswords have been incapacitated by the traps, but even when it's one against many, Keith fights coolly with a short sword in each hand. His motions are sharp and as choreographed as a sword dance. Since he wears spectacles, Aileen assumed he was a civil servant–type with poor eyesight, but apparently, that isn't the case. Reconsidering, she decides he's really more like a spy.

"I can do that much."

For some reason, Beelzebuth interjects, looking irritated.

"I've told you again and again—the demons must not fight," Aileen reminds him.

"...Then when do I get my turn?"

"Possibly during the last battle between humans and demons? Either that, or against demons."

In the distance, she sees lights. It's the band of knights the other party has summoned to capture Keith. However, she's asked her father to switch out about half of them. Now that the demons have fled and the client is unconscious, all Keith has to do is say,

I've prevented the sale of demons, without the demon king's knowledge, and this farce will be over. Even in the game, the duty the emperor gave Lilia and the others was not to find the culprit, but to settle the matter peacefully.

Was that because the emperor wanted to see how well Master Cedric and the others could negotiate? This is an incredibly knotty problem, after all. There is the whole question of what to do regarding the relationship with Master Claude.

Looking down over the scene, she remembers something: *Come to think of it, why haven't Lilia and the others shown up?*

Even though silencing those three seems likely to be the most troublesome part of this—

"Aileen!"

"!!"

She hears a shout, and a brown-skinned arm pulls her in close. Then there's a nasty hissing noise and the smell of something scorching.

"Beelzebuth?! You're...!"

From the shoulder down, his arm has been hideously burned. Breaking out in a greasy sweat, Beelzebuth falls to his knees, and Aileen hastily slips free of his arm. Just then, three figures appear.

"Oh—oh no. What should I do? I only meant to keep him at bay, so he wouldn't attack, but I..."

"It's fine; you only scratched him. You're not to blame, Lilia."

"...Master Cedric."

"Get behind me, you two. Aileen's skills aren't half bad."

"Marcus."

And finally, Aileen looks up at the girl. It's from the same angle she saw her on that earlier day.

"Lady Lilia..."

"It's all right, Lady Aileen. We only want to talk to you."

The Maid of the Sacred Sword smiles sweetly.

The sacred sword of legend in Imperial Ellmeyer is a shining blade that can destroy the demon king with a single stroke. It's said to have materialized from the body of the maiden who routed the demons and founded the country. It changes its shape in response to the will of its wielder and can become an enormous sword that pierces the very heavens. The light particles it emits burn demons.

However, in the long history of Imperial Ellmeyer, the only woman ever to possess that sacred sword is the Maid. The imperial and ducal families had continued her bloodline, so that some-day, a maiden who possessed the sacred sword would be born. However, in the end, Lilia ended up in possession of the sword, as the reincarnation of the Maid.

The Maid naturally wields the sword in order to drive away the demon hordes and defend humanity. In order to bring peace to the world.

"Come with us, please, Lady Aileen."

"...In the middle of the night? If you're requesting a visit, wouldn't daytime be more suitable?"

"Aileen, run."

On his knees, panting shallowly, Beelzebuth speaks in a hoarse voice. She wraps her arms around him, shielding him, and responds softly.

"No, you run, Beelzebuth. Hurry and have Master Claude treat that wound—!!"

"No unnecessary talking."

Someone grabs her by the scruff of her neck and drags her away. Beelzebuth raises his head.

"Aileen!"

"I'm fine, just hurry and run! I'll handle this on my own somehow— No! Don't!"

Seeing Lilia aim the sacred sword at Beelzebuth, she grabs her hand. Immediately, Marcus hooks his arm around Aileen's neck from behind, squeezing it. Even so, desperate to distract Lilia, she shouts:

"I'm the one you want, right?! Besides, if you kill a demon, you'll have violated the nonaggression pact. Do you intend to bring the emperor's wrath down upon yourselves?"

Lilia's eyebrows twitch. The fact that she's still smiling makes the gesture incredibly unsettling.

Did something happen with the emperor? ...In the first place, if this is playing out like the game event, it should be Master Keith they're after.

Aileen doesn't understand. The only thing that's certain is that this development wasn't in the game.

"It's all right. We won't do anything awful to you, Lady Aileen."

"I feel as if I've already been humiliated quite enough."

"I'm the one who's being humiliated. But I must endure it. After all, Cedric's in trouble..."

Lilia lowers her eyelashes in a melancholy way. As if to console her, Cedric hugs her shoulders. Then he looks at Aileen, who's been restrained by Marcus, and gives an oddly gentle smile.

"Be glad. I'm going to make you my consort. This very night."

"...Huh? What...are you—?!"

"Wait! Let Aileen go...!"

Using the weapon Denis gave him as a cane, Beelzebuth rises to his feet.

Lilia draws her eyebrows together, as if she's troubled.

"Um, I don't particularly want to attack you, but…"

"That woman is someone precious."

Beelzebuth reaches out for Aileen.

"She's the king's precious woman!"

"Getting that desperate isn't going to… You'll be no match for the sacred sword, you know? Besides, you're a demon. Isn't it odd for you to say a human is precious?"

A dry *smack* rings out. Aileen has slapped Lilia across the face.

Marcus goes pale. Still restraining Aileen, he backs up hastily.

"Aileen, how could you do that to Lilia?!"

"Beelzebuth, go back. Go to Master Claude. I—"

Glaring at Lilia, who's standing dazed, one hand to her struck cheek, Aileen makes a declaration.

"I'll never lose to a woman who treated you with contempt!"

"Aileen!"

A solid impact runs through the side of her head, and the world spins sickeningly, going dark. Was it Cedric who hit her? The last thing she sees, dimly, is Beelzebuth's shocked face.

It's all right, though. He'll think of the best move, then act accordingly. She has full faith that he will do what's right.

With every wingbeat, fierce pain shoots through him. It feels as though all his strength is being taken from him through that wound.

Even so, he desperately searches his surroundings, peering

through the darkness. According to the plan, that fellow should be nearby, preparing to deal with the aftermath.

Hurry, hurry. At this speed, it's going to take time to reach the forest. His strength may fail him before he gets there, and so, and so—

There he is. The human!

"Beelzebuth?! You're wounded!"

"D-Denis... Never mind...me. Aileen was..."

"Luc! Come here, please. Beelzebuth is—"

"No, just...listen."

He grabs his arm tightly. As he supports Beelzebuth with his own small frame, Denis looks straight at him.

"They took Aileen. There were three of them. One was at that human soiree..."

"Three... Lady Lilia, Master Cedric, and Master Marcus?"

"Right, the names were...something like that... Hurry..."

"Denis! What's—? That wound—you've been seared clear through...! A-at any rate, let's get you first aid. Quartz, mix this and bring some water!"

Apparently, they've put some kind of salve on him. For a moment, a new fierce pain courses through him, dragging his awareness back. A cool sensation follows, and the pain subsides a little.

"Heeey! We managed to dupe the knights just fine— Whoa, what happened?!"

"Jasper, good. Where's Isaac? It sounds as if Master Cedric and the others have kidnapped Miss Aileen!"

"Huh?! What the hell for?"

"...To be his second wife, he said..."

Breathing roughly, Beelzebuth barely manages to squeeze the

words out. He doesn't know anything beyond that. However, the man in the beret puts a hand to his mouth, casting around for the answer.

"Wait, was that actually for real? The one about how folk are concerned that Lady Lilia doesn't have the capacity to be empress, so if he at least makes Miss Aileen his second wife…"

"Huh? So why would he kidnap her? Is he stupid? He should just propose openly and get shot down in style— Beelzebuth, this is going to sting a little. Denis, give him some water to drink."

"Prime Minister d'Autriche is adamantly against it. Some of the aristocrats who saw her dance with the demon king at that soiree have begun to talk about reverting the title of crown prince to Master Claude instead… Uh, anyway, I'm gonna go fill Isaac in. Then we'll figure out exactly what's going on and work out a plan."

"Please do!"

"Thank…you."

It must be relief at the conversation he's overheard. Unexpected words slip from him.

"I…ran."

"Beelzebuth…"

"It wasn't that I feared the sacred sword. If it would have saved her, I wouldn't have minded dying. However, I thought…I couldn't save her…on my own."

"—Yeah, and you were right about that."

The droplets spilling from his eyes keep him from seeing the speaker clearly.

"You did good. I'd expect no less from the demon king's right-hand man. The sacred sword didn't even make you flinch."

"…Isaac."

"You people are loud. I heard all that. Mister, send a report to the demon king. For now, don't tell that assassin-type attendant of his; it'll just complicate everything— Well, you know the demon king's probably gonna go save her anyway. That means our job is to get the prep work done, then clean up afterward.

"...In the meantime..." The mere human has the gall to lay a hand over his eyelids. "...Get some sleep. It's all right. By the time you wake up, Aileen's gonna be badgering the demon king to marry her again."

I see. I hope so.

After all, if Aileen is by his king's side, there will be a place for him there as well.

She hears the sound of scraping metal.

Pain lances through her temple. She can feel that her hair is sticky and clinging to her scalp. It's probably blood.

"—All right, Lilia. Let's go. There's no space in this tower. It would be better to go relax over there."

"Yes, you're...right. Cedric...um..."

"Lilia. Please understand. In order to ensure your happiness, I must be crown prince. It's only this once. You will be my principal wife."

"Oh...Lady Aileen is awake."

Lilia smiles, the tears summarily vanishing from her eyes as she looks up at Cedric.

Aileen draws a deep breath, then calls to them.

"...And just what is the meaning of this?"

There are iron shackles on her wrists, and the chain that extends from them is wrapped around the bedpost. She can't move.

—That's right; Aileen is lying on a bed. Her wrists are bound over her head.

"I'll forgive you for what you did earlier. After all, I'm sure you were confused, Lady Aileen."

Putting a hand to her own cheek, which is no longer red, Lilia offers her a delicate smile.

"You may not believe me, but I do genuinely respect you. Let's do our best together."

"What is this talk of 'second wives' and 'together'? As I'm sure you're aware, my engagement to Master Cedric has been dissolved. Thanks to none other than you yourself."

"That's true, but I'm really not very good at talking to sordid nobles who play along with crafty lies and deceive one another... However, you have a particular talent for it, don't you, Lady Aileen? I'd like you to help me."

Aileen has begun to see where this is going.

Due to Lilia's thoughtless behavior at that soiree, her suitability as empress—and by extension, Cedric's suitability as crown prince—has probably come into question. While Lilia is the daughter of a baron, her family doesn't have much political power to speak of. People have begun to openly look down on them for that, and so these two must have had a really dim-witted idea.

They'd push the job of empress and all the onerous duties onto Aileen, thus securing their own positions.

"Help you, hmm? —Lady Lilia, you don't have the slightest intention of doing actual work for Master Cedric's sake, do you?"

"Oh, no, that's not... It's just, everyone has their strengths and weaknesses."

"It's fine, Lilia. I never planned to force you to go along with old, formal customs anyway."

"You sound like a child going through a rebellious phase. What did the emperor say to that particular statement?"

Cedric and Lilia are at a complete loss for words, and their reactions make the answer obvious: The emperor refused to take them seriously.

"—Marcus. Take Lilia and go."

Marcus puts an arm around Lilia's shoulders, and she leaves the room. The heavy iron door appears to be the only exit. She even hears them lock it. Barring it from the inside on top of that, Cedric sits down on the side of the bed.

He looks down at Aileen, his eyes cold—and abruptly, he grabs her by the collar, putting his face right in front of her nose.

"I've been thinking all this time. How long have you and my brother been together?"

"...What are you saying?"

"I wonder why Father said a woman as wanton as you was suited to be empress. He finally told me that if I insisted on Lilia, I should get myself a concubine who was fit for the role of an emperor's consort."

"So now you're trying to get back together with me? But then why imprison me? What do you—?"

Partway through, it hits her, and she falls silent.

A way to make me his second wife, this very night.

There certainly is one. If that happens to her, Aileen will have no choice but to marry Cedric.

After all, in this country, the daughters of the nobility have a duty to continue the line of the imperial family.

"Mmph, ghk!"

"I won't be able to get in the mood if you're noisy. I don't want to make Lilia listen to that, either, and I can't have you biting your tongue."

Cedric has pulled out his handkerchief and tied it around her head, forcing it into her mouth like a gag. Then, using a small knife, he cuts the laces that fasten Aileen's dress at the front and the fabric along with them. He's almost businesslike about it.

"Nnnnn! Nnnnn!"

"If I sleep with you now, you'll be my second wife. Then I'll be able to get Duke d'Autriche to back me. If anyone gets in my way, it will be my brother— Still, I wonder what kind of face he'll make?"

She struggles, flailing with her legs. As Cedric leans over her, she kicks him solidly in the gut.

Eyes blazing with anger, Cedric straddles Aileen and strikes her on the cheek. Then he hits the other one. And then again.

"Even I! Don't want to do! A thing like this! Why don't you understand?!"

"......!"

"You're going to be useful to the man you loved. Be grateful...!"

He tears the fabric around her neck savagely. *I want to buy time, at least*, she thinks.

Or would it be more sensible to give some calm thought to how best to behave after this?

After this—

Before she can think, she turns pale. If Claude finds out...

She cut her mouth when he'd hit her, and the taste of blood is already spreading.

She's sure Claude won't reject her just for this. Even so, she worries she won't be able to keep that beautiful demon king's eyes from seeing her as damaged.

The thought is impossible to bear. Even more than that, it startles her.

To think that she, Aileen Lauren d'Autriche, would care about the gaze of that single man. The idea that she'd want to be at her very purest in his mind.

Anyone would suspect she is in love.

—In that case, you really must do something about this situation! Pull yourself together!

She's frozen up, and she scolds herself sharply for it. This thing that's crawling on top of her isn't much different from a caterpillar. There's no way a human should lose to that. That means there's absolutely no reason for her to give up or to cry.

"Gwuff!"

Since she'd stopped moving, Cedric got the mistaken impression that she decided to behave, and she nails him again... However, that's all.

I should have had Mother teach me how to kill a man with my feet!

"W-would you—! Give up—! And behave alre—?"

"Here! Demon king, I found Aileen!!"

She looks in the direction of the muffled voice. A crow is plastered against the iron bars of the window. She can just make out the bow tie on his neck. It's Almond.

She widens her eyes, and in the same moment, the ceiling blows off. Her field of view expands all at once.

Master Claude.

The figure that's descended from the lavender night sky is a king who won't lose to anyone, as long as he's human.

Relief fills her chest. There's no frustration or pride there. Finally, trembling begins to work its way up from deep inside her, and tears spill across the cheek that's turned to the bed. She sobs.

He came to save me.

It's all right. There's nothing to be afraid of now.

But there's something Aileen hasn't realized.

How this situation must look to Claude.

A blast of wind whips through. Unable even to scream, Cedric tries to curl up on the bed, covering his head—but the gale promptly sends him flying. He crashes into the wall, then slumps to the floor.

"H-hurting a human— Brothe—"

"How...dare..."

She could swear that she just heard a light crack. Claude shrinks back, covering half his face. Thick scales have begun to cover that hand.

Finally, Aileen registers what's happening.

The "demon king's awakening" event! But we avoided that! Why...? No. Don't tell me...

A precious woman. Beelzebuth's words come back to her. In other words—

"Cedric! What happened?!"

"Lilia! Hurry, the sacred sword! It's just as we thought: Anger turns him into a demon. We did it!"

Lilia has clambered in through the half-demolished wall, and Cedric clings to her. Aileen, who'd been left stunned by her fresh realization, quickly comes back to her senses.

Anger toward humans. Just like despair, it makes Claude harbor malice.

And what makes her want to click her tongue in irritation is the significance behind the fact that Cedric and the others wanted this to happen.

If Master Claude becomes a demon, it will be nothing but good news for those three!

If Lilia kills the demon king, she will solidly establish herself as the saint who saved the empire. No one will dare say she isn't fit to be empress. On the contrary, the people might go as far as venerating and serving her as a ruling empress, rather than a mere emperor's consort.

"Nnnnn! Nnnnn!"

Aileen calls out to Almond, who's been pulled into the whirlwind and is desperately holding his own.

Hearing her, Almond comes over and pecks at the shackles. *Your beak isn't going to do a thing*, she thinks, but she should have expected more from a demon; he brings his beak down in one decisive stroke, and they shatter.

Using her now freed hands, she unties the handkerchief gag.

"What...did you...do to Aileen?"

Even as Aileen works herself free, Claude's transformation has continued, with sounds like panes of glass shattering one by one. As if he's shedding his human existence, scales spread across his arms, his nails lengthen, and his hands morph into forelegs.

"What did you...? She's my... Ah—ah, *ah*—"

"Master Claude! I'm fine, so please calm yourself!"

Their eyes meet. Claude widens his large red eyes, and he takes a step back.

"Don't…look."

That gesture, as if he's ashamed of himself, stops her in her tracks.

"…Please don't…look. I was…trying to save you, but—"

"Demon king."

The voice rings out like a holy bell that repels demons.

Light gleams. It's the radiance of the sacred sword. The saint's sword that passes judgment on the demon king.

"You poor thing. It must be painful, having to constantly stifle your emotions. The woman who's precious to you has been hurt, and you can't even let yourself get angry? There's nothing human about that."

The saint smiles nobly and cruelly. With no hesitation, Aileen rushes toward the tip of her sword.

"I'll put an end to your sorrow—!"

Is it the light of the rising sun or the holy light that will kill the demon king?

Right in front of Aileen, Lilia's eyes go wide.

In her hands is the sacred sword. About half that sword is buried in Aileen.

"—I apologize for taking you lightly. I'm dense. To think I didn't even realize I was being targeted. I'm in no position to laugh at Master Keith."

"Uhhh… Le-let go!"

Lilia tries to move her hands, attempting to pull the sword out of Aileen, but Aileen grabs her wrists, and she doesn't let go.

"Wh-what are you thinking? The sacred sword may not work on humans, but this is…!"

"What…are you saying…? It's excruciating…!! The part about it not…working on humans…had better be true…"

Is this the sort of pain one feels when one is stabbed through the stomach? If she coughed up blood, would she feel better?

Smile. You mustn't let her feel the tiniest bit superior about having gotten you. From start to finish, her policy will not change.

"Listen... What do you suppose happens if the sacred sword stabs a human?"

"Huh?! Wh-what happens? How should I—?"

"A saint who stabs a human with it might disqualify herself as the Maid— And what if the one she's stabbed... is of the bloodline of...the Maid of the Sacred Sword?"

Lilia widens her eyes. It's just as she suspected: This woman isn't stupid.

"I won't let you kill Master Claude. I'm taking the sacred sword."

Planting her feet firmly, she pulls Lilia's hands toward herself.

Light bursts forth. The sword sinks into her, deeper and deeper. However, its tip never emerges from her back. It continues entering Aileen's body, accompanied by ferocious pain.

"C-Cedric! Marcus! Do something about Lady Aileen!"

"Almond!"

All Aileen has to do is call his name, and Almond and his companions fly to obstruct Cedric and Marcus. They flap around them, blocking their vision, but are careful not to hurt them. The sight makes her smile.

"Y-you're insane! This isn't...!"

When the sword is buried up to the hilt, she's practically pressed against Lilia. Right in front of her nose, even as she breaks out in a greasy sweat, Aileen smiles at her.

"You're not the protagonist of this story. I am."

Lilia gasps. Shoving her away, Aileen finishes burying the

sword with her own hands. Stifling a scream, she swallows down the ferocious pain—and then the sensation abruptly vanishes.

Having lost the sacred sword, Lilia backs away, shaking her head as if she's terribly frightened. Aileen doesn't bother with her. She turns around.

Under the dim sky, there's an enormous, pitch-black dragon. Its lovely red eyes are wide and stunned. Reflected in those jewel-like eyes, Aileen gives a musical laugh.

"My, Master Claude. You are quite dashing, aren't you?"

"......"

"I wouldn't mind keeping you like this, either, but…it would make married life rather difficult, don't you think?"

As she speaks, she softly leans against the hard scales of his chest. She closes her eyes.

"Thank you for coming to my rescue. I felt so relieved that I cried. You wicked man. You made me cry quite handily, didn't you? You'll have to take responsibility for that."

She's able to believe it will be all right. There's no way the game Lilia could do something she can't do.

After all, she shouldn't have had a chance of conquering the final boss, and yet here she is.

"You needn't give up on anything, Master Claude."

What comes after this will be unscripted, and even the happiness of humans and demons living together is a dream she'll make come true.

"Come now. If you love me, come back."

Dawn breaks, ending that terrible night, and as if a spell is coming undone, the scales turn into light, then scatter.

When she slowly opens her eyes, the black-haired, red-eyed, infuriatingly beautiful demon king stands before her once more.

In front of an alabaster altar surrounded by columns, the black-haired demon king alights.

This is the place where the Maid of the Sacred Sword once held that blade high and proclaimed the kingdom's foundation. It's also where Claude once surrendered his right to inherit the throne.

"Claude Jean Ellmeyer. I hereby name you crown prince."

Verifying the document that has been signed before the altar, the emperor's proxy, Prime Minister Rudolph Lauren d'Autriche, makes a proclamation of his own.

"Aileen Lauren d'Autriche."

"Yes."

With graceful steps, Aileen advances to the center of the space. Claude turns slightly to look at her.

"I pronounce your betrothal to Crown Prince Claude, as the empress-elect."

"I humbly accept."

She responds with a flawless noblewoman's curtsy. Cheers and congratulatory applause go up, and flower petals fill the air. Of course, there are various thoughts behind these events. This is the human world, after all.

That's exactly why I'm needed. Aileen starts down the aisle, where petals flutter and drift, in order to go to Claude. Then she spots Cedric and the others, in attendance off to the side.

Without restraining herself, she flashes them an elegant smile.

"Why, *Second Prince* Cedric. Have you come to congratulate me?"

Cedric doesn't respond, but now that he's been demoted to second prince, his expression is clearly stiff. Lilia is standing beside him; she doesn't look up. Marcus, who's accompanying them, is glaring at Aileen with something close to murder in his eyes. No doubt they'd have preferred to be absent.

However, if they wanted to pretend as if nothing had happened, they'd had no choice but to attend Claude's investiture as crown prince—the ceremony where his right to inherit would be restored—and congratulate him, as etiquette demanded.

"Master Claude has been removed from the political arena for quite some time. Please do support him, as his subjects. As one who will someday be empress, I will do my utmost as well."

As before, there's no reply. Apparently, Cedric is nothing more than a sore loser. Aileen chuckles, wearing a victor's smile.

"Aileen."

Possibly because it seems to be taking her forever to reach him, Claude comes to her.

"What are you doing? We're going home."

"Oh, already?"

"The demons are worried. Also, I don't intend to put myself on display."

Catching her by surprise, he puts a hand on her waist and pulls her to him. For a moment, she feels the urge to struggle, but she curbs it. Embarrassing her fiancé in public must be avoided at all costs. She limits her resistance to furtively glaring at Claude.

Her feet lift lightly off the ground. As the day's central figures rise into the air, a stir runs through the assembled crowd.

However, Aileen collects herself, smiles elegantly, and wraps an arm around Claude's neck, as he hugs her to his side.

A carriage that races through the night sky is marvelous, but so is looking down over an astonished crowd from high in the air.

"All right. Good day to you, everyone."

With a *snap*, Aileen and Claude vanish. Afterward, Cedric fervently protests the idea of making the demon king crown prince, a tearful Lilia relates how she lost the sacred sword, and Marcus defends them both. *"They were terribly wretched, and it was all very entertaining,"* Rudolph tells Aileen later on.

"So bottom line: We can take our time and crush those three idiots later. Just leave it to me; I'll make them universal laughingstocks."

"Your plans are even less merciful, aren't they, Isaac?"

"Ha-ha. He's our resident problem-solver, so that's probably only to be expected."

"...He lost the rank of crown prince, and she's had the position of saint taken from her. I think they're laughingstocks already."

"So do I, but I doubt things will stay that peaceful. Here, take a look at this article. It seems like there's gonna be a power struggle over whether to side with the forbidden first prince and his demonic loyalties or the second prince, who's incompetent but indisputably human."

"Why are you people sitting idle?"

Aileen has entered the conference room, and at the sight of the five of them lazing around the table, she draws herself up and plants her hand on her hips.

"Hurry and get to work. We haven't yet repaid the entire sum

I borrowed from Father to purchase the land. I'd really rather not stay in his debt if we can help it. Isaac, how are our sales?"

"They've doubled, due to the offer with the cosmetic case. It may be time to think about whether we should have a store."

"Denis, how are the castle repairs and remodeling coming along?"

"Just about done! Beelzebuth's wounds are healed up, and he's been helping us out a lot."

"Aileen!"

The conference room door opens with a bang, and in walks the demon himself.

"What, you're still working? You promised you'd read this book."

"Wait just a little longer. If you have time, why don't you read the book I read the other day to the demons? That will help you review as well."

Beelzebuth has recently begun learning to read. He nods obediently, reminds her about her promise once more, and leaves. As he watches him go, Isaac speaks up.

"...Hey, Denis. When did that demon start calling Aileen by name?"

"Huh? Now that you mention it... Miss Aileen's stopped being formal with him, too."

"How is he, Miss Aileen? Is he a quick learner?"

"In terms of learning the letters, Almond is faster."

She responds with a straight face, and the rest of them look rather awkward.

Clearing his throat, Jasper changes the subject.

"What about that other attendant? I haven't seen him around lately. Don't tell me he's quit."

"Master Keith is buying back demons at a ferocious pace. He's started to make unscrupulous proposals to Master Claude without a blush, too; he's impossible to deal with anymore."

"He's incredible at maneuvering, isn't he? They'll be building a school in the fifth layer soon, and I hear he's the one who arranged for it."

Luc's information is news to her. Quartz adds to it.

"...The demon king is financing it."

"Wait just a minute. Don't tell me—is that funding coming from our coffers?! Isaac!"

"Philanthropic work is vital to our future business. It's fiiiine, I'll be clever about it."

"Yes, but even so— Almond!"

Aileen's sharp eyes have spotted the crow, who's crept out of her shadow and is attempting to scrounge through the snacks on the conference room shelves. She glares at him.

"How many times must I tell you to stop sneaking food? It's bad manners. Do you want to be burned by the sacred sword?"

"I'll tell the demon king on you!"

"For your information, at this point, I could crush Master Claude with a single attack as well."

"This is why you get called the Maid of the Cursed Sword..."

"The demon king is human, so the sacred sword won't work on him, correct?"

"Don't go crushing him with sex appeal."

At Isaac's offhanded comment, Aileen smacks the round table.

"Never mind, just get to work, all of you! I have something to discuss with Master Claude."

"""""Okaaaay.""""" With their drawled response ringing in her ears, Aileen leaves the conference room.

Honestly! We can't afford to get complacent. After all, the real struggle is only just beginning.

It has been a month since the event in which Claude nearly awakened as the demon king.

In exchange for not pressing charges against Cedric for abducting and imprisoning her, Aileen negotiated with the emperor to have Claude's right to inherit reinstated. The information Isaac and the others had gathered in the brief time before her rescue was so complete that no evasions were possible, and so it might have been more accurate to say she threatened rather than negotiated. The one who did the actual communicating was Rudolph, but apparently, he had almost no trouble at all.

She'd been concerned that Claude himself might refuse this arrangement, but as it turned out, her worry was for nothing. Possibly due to the backlash from acquiring the sacred sword, Aileen had been confined to her bed, and when Claude came to visit her, Rudolph told him, *"I will marry Aileen to whoever becomes emperor."* Claude responded, apparently with no hesitation at all, *"Then I will become emperor."*

When she heard that, Aileen was reduced to writhing and rolling around on her bed for a while, but that's a story for another time.

Now that Claude has taken up his duties as the crown prince, the castle's parlor room has been converted into an office. When Aileen peeks into it, Claude looks up.

"Just a moment. I'm almost done."

Of course. Aileen nods, obediently taking a seat on the sofa. Claude writes rapidly with his quill, and once he's finished, he snaps his fingers, sending the document to the courier. How convenient.

Claude has turned into a demon once, and yet in the end, he's living the same way he did before, as a human and the demon king. Aileen is proud of him.

After all, it means he'll be able to gain happiness both as the demon king and as a human.

"Well? What is it?"

"I've found humans who will be good teachers for the demons, and I'm considering bringing them here. What do you think?" Aileen asks.

"You're collecting more...?" Claude wonders in exasperation.

"Of course. We have far too few human allies. We need to gather good talent."

"That wasn't what I meant, but... Well, do as you wish. If necessary, I'll handle it somehow."

He sighs as he speaks, and her eyebrows twitch.

"What do you mean by that? You speak as if I am in constant need of your protection, Master Claude."

"What's wrong with protecting the woman who will someday be my wife?"

This time, still smiling, she freezes up. Claude sets his elbows on his ebony work desk, resting his chin in his hands.

"Being my wife also means charmingly allowing yourself to be protected. I've earned at least that much. You aren't yet sufficiently conscious of that."

He's not wrong. However.

"...You sound as if you're enjoying yourself."

"The thought that you're probably vexed is incredibly entertaining."

You don't have to be so honest about that. As she's inwardly gritting her teeth, her body rises lightly. Aileen has become the Maid of the Sacred Sword, but perhaps because she stole the sword, Claude's magic affects her just as it would a normal human if she isn't paying attention.

Even so, falling into his lap when she's unable to struggle doesn't sit well with her.

Scowling, Aileen tries to stand, but Claude easily holds her close. She knows he'll be amused if she reacts, but even so, when he kisses the back of her neck, her temperature skyrockets.

"You are at work! Have you no shame, Master Claude?!"

"I can't get enough of the fact that you never seem to get used to this."

"Wh-why do you sound like a demon king more than ever? Stop that...!"

"If you dislike demon kings, I would advise you to run."

If she's careless, Claude's hands will get up to some outrageous mischief, so she's been holding them down. However, at his teasing whisper, she looks up, irked. Rising to his provocation, she resettles herself heavily on Claude's lap.

"Run? You do say such strange things."

Even if Claude has been reinstated as crown prince, it doesn't change the fact that he's the demon king. Humans who fear the demons are bound to promote Cedric and rally around him. The fact that Lilia used to be the Maid of the Sacred Sword will only spur them on.

For Claude, the road to the imperial throne certainly won't be a smooth one.

However, nonchalantly stomping on hardships and crushing them underfoot is what makes life enjoyable.

—And most of all.

"I'm the one who caught you. I have no intention of letting you get away."

Not him, or life, or happiness, or her dream of becoming empress, or her second love.

Imperial Ellmeyer was founded by the Maid of the Sacred Sword, who once slew the demon king.

The Maid of the Cursed Sword—having vanquished the Maid of the Sacred Sword—now strives to make the demon king the emperor, and what follows is her story.

Afterword

It's either a pleasure to meet you or it's been a while since we last met. My name is Sarasa Nagase. Thank you very much for picking up my humble attempt at a novel.

This story was originally posted and serialized online, and now they've been kind enough to turn it into a physical book for me. It's the first time I've ever had a story that's already been posted online published as a book, so I'm excited.

No major changes have been made between this and the online version, but there are places that are different here and there, so it would make me happy if you had fun comparing the two.

And now for the thank-yous.

To Mai Murasaki, who drew the illustrations: I could never fully express how grateful I am to you for drawing Aileen as an adorable beauty, and particularly for making Claude—who's constantly being referred to as *gorgeous* in the text—a great demon king who shines brightly in the darkness. Thank you very much.

To my supervising editor: As it turns out, I ended up causing you the same sort of trouble as usual. Thank you very much for adjusting my schedule for me when things were already very tight.

To the proofreaders, the members of the editorial department, the designers and marketing personnel, the staff at the printer, and everyone who was involved in the making of this book: I'm deeply grateful to you.

To everyone who's been reading this story since the online version: It's thanks to you that Aileen and company have been published in book format, complete with illustrations. Thank you so much for your support.

Finally, to everyone who picked up this book: Thank you very much for sticking with me this far. If reading this story entertains you in some small way, I'll be very happy.

Now then, with prayers that we'll meet again...

Sarasa Nagase